Lily Vanessa and the Pet Panic

The
Twelve Candles Club

9610

Lily Vanessa and the Pet Panic

Elaine L. Schulte

BETHANY HOUSE PUBLISHERS
MINNEAPOLIS, MINNESOTA 55438

Published by Bethany House Publishers
A Ministry of Bethany Fellowship, Inc.
11300 Hampshire Avenue South
Minneapolis, Minnesota 55438

Printed in the United States of America.

Library of Congress Cataloging-in-Publication Data

Schulte, Elaine L.
 Lily Vanessa and the pet panic / Elaine L. Schulte.
  p. cm. — (The Twelve Candles club ; #11)
 Summary: While staying with relatives in southern California, Lily
Vanessa wonders if the Twelve Candles Club will accept a black girl as
a member, but as they work on a variety of jobs and ask her to sing at
their church, Lily knows that Jesus has helped her make new friends.
 [1. Christian life—Fiction. 2. Clubs—Fiction. 3. Moneymaking
projects—Fiction. 4. Afro-Americans—Fiction.] I. Title.
II. Series. III. Series: Schulte, Elaine L. Twelve Candles Club ; 11.
PZ7. S3867Li 1996
[Fic]—dc21   96–45835
ISBN 1–55661–539–6   CIP
                  AC

With gratitude for suggestions from
Tiffany Anderson
Amanda Harris
Lin Harris
Mary Huckstep
Gladys Johnson
Courtney Mason
Candice McAdams
Janet McCaulie
Lydia Richardson
Susan Richardson
Bob Rose
Jonah Schrowang
Russ Schrowang
Donna Schroeder
Nell Sunukjian
Andrea Taylor
Marisa Williams

ELAINE L. SCHULTE is the well-known author of thirty-six novels for women and children. Over one million copies of her popular books have been sold. She received a Distinguished Alumna Award from Purdue University as well as numerous other awards for her work as an author. After living in various places, including several years in Europe, she and her husband make their home in Fallbrook, California, where she writes full time.

CHAPTER

1

Lily Vanessa Shields held the red plastic cat cage well aside so Cat's fleas wouldn't jump out on her. "Hold still, Cat. Hold still! I feel peculiar enough as it is."

It was more than the hot gusts of Southern California winds that made her feel peculiar. Here she was—a tall, skinny, twelve-year-old black girl strolling along in her aunt and uncle's mostly white neighborhood—and feeling as if something strange and exciting might happen.

All she knew so far about the Twelve Candles Club girls was that they baby-sat and did other work all over Santa Rosita. But maybe they'd know the owner of this white-furred cat with big orange and black splotches who made Uncle Raymond's eyes swell up with allergies.

"Me-owwww!" Cat complained loudly.

"Me-owwww, yourself!" Lily Vanessa answered, exasperated. It had been a royal battle getting Cat out of the laundry room and into the cage. "Me-ow!"

Meowing back made her feel braver about finding a home for Cat. Sure, Aunt Van and Uncle Raymond lived in Santa Rosita Estates, but it wasn't like her more ethnically mixed Los Angeles neighborhood, just a two-hour drive north.

She glanced ahead to the Bennett house.

Yes-s!

Her timing was perfect, thanks to her aunt's suggestion to arrive exactly at noon. The little kids—Funners—were being picked up by their parents from the Twelve Candles Club's morning playcare.

Lily Vanessa slowed her long feet, watching as the Funners climbed into their parents' cars and vans. Doors slammed and three more cars drove up.

Filled with kids, the cars and minivans finally drove away and only the TCC girls—all twelve years old, too—stood talking on the driveway. They wore cutoffs and tees, just like hers except for the colors. Today she wore her blue-green tee; theirs were peach, blue, green, yellow, and purple.

Lily Vanessa called out, "Hi! Do you know who this cat belongs to?"

The five girls swung around in surprise.

Lily Vanessa added, "She doesn't have a collar."

The short, sturdy girl wearing a peach-colored T-shirt with the name JESS on it saw her and hesitated. Finally, she gave her a smile and looked at the cage. "Hey, that's a beautiful cat."

The others had already looked Lily Vanessa over, and now they stepped closer to eye Cat.

"Pfitts!" Cat hissed at them. "Pffffittttttttttttttts!"

"Yow! Beautiful but ornery!" said the JESS T-shirt girl. "She's probably a stray. It seems like there are always strays around here. Probably one stray a week."

"That's what my aunt and uncle said," Lily Vanessa answered. "I looked for its owners all last week."

"Where did you look?" the JESS T-shirt girl asked.

"I checked for 'Lost Cat' signs tacked to mailboxes and light poles, even in the *Santa Rosita Times* classified ads."

"How about the animal shelter?" another girl asked.

Lily Vanessa nodded. "My aunt phoned them right away, and I phoned again this morning. They haven't had any calls for a lost cat who looks anything like this one."

Just then, Cat raked a paw with gleaming claws at her, and Lily Vanessa jerked back fast.

"Whoa!" the girls yelled.

" 'Whoa' is right," Lily Vanessa said as she plopped the cage in the shade on the driveway.

Ignoring Cat's hissing and spitting, she turned to the girls. "I'm Lily Vanessa Shields. I'm staying over at my Aunt Van and Uncle Raymond's on La Fortuna for two weeks while my mom's away at a meeting for school principals. My dad's a captain in the navy. He's stationed in Italy right now."

She rushed on, wishing she didn't sound so nervous. "Usually I live in L.A. You know, Los Angeles. I go back next week to get ready for school."

"I'm Jess McColl," said the girl in the peach T-shirt. "Four of us live on this street. And this is Becky Hamilton, our Twelve Candles Club's president. She just moved across town."

The tall girl in the blue tee stepped forward, and Lily Vanessa blurted, "Hey, you have long feet, too! Oops—"

Becky glanced at their feet and gave a laugh. "That's a fact!" Still smiling, she added, "We didn't know you were staying in the neighborhood. Umm . . . this is Tricia Bennett, who lives here. . . ."

Tricia . . . the blondish redhead, green tee, like her eyes, Lily Vanessa thought, trying to fix the name Tricia in her head.

" . . . and Melanie Lin . . ."

Melanie . . . pretty Asian girl . . . purple tee. . . .

" . . . Cara Hernandez . . ."

Cara . . . dark hair, brown eyes, Hispanic features . . . a little shy . . . yellow tee. . . .

They were eying her, too, probably thinking, *tall, skinny black girl with long feet, blue-green tee, and a headful of cornrow braids.* Did they expect something exciting to happen, too?

"My aunt told me about your club," Lily Vanessa said. "I thought, since you know so many people, maybe you'd know the owner of this cat."

Tricia shook her head. "No, and I haven't heard of anyone missing a cat."

Lily Vanessa shrugged helplessly.

Tricia hesitated, then asked, "Hey, why don't you have lunch with us? Mom's making hot dogs. You could phone your aunt to ask—"

"Thanks! I'd love to have lunch with you," Lily Vanessa answered with amazement. "My aunt's at a school meeting, and Uncle Raymond's at work, so I'm on my own." She picked up Cat's cage. "My aunt teaches at Santa Rosita Middle School—"

"That's where we're going in a week!" Cara interrupted. "Except Becky. What's your aunt's name?"

"Mrs. Williams. She teaches English."

Tricia led them to her wooden breezeway gate and opened it wide. "Maybe she'll be our teacher. What's she like?"

Lily Vanessa considered her aunt. "Firm but nice, I'd guess. She loves poetry."

"Great, so do I," Cara said, not so shy now. "In fact, I was remembering a poem about cats. 'Cat! Scat! Off her mat . . .' Oops, I don't remember the rest. Something about 'green-eyed scratcher.' "

"Sounds good anyhow," Lily Vanessa assured her. "I'm not very poetic, even though Aunt Van keeps working on me. Seems like grown-ups are always trying to improve kids."

"You said it," Becky answered.

As they made their way through the Bennetts' breezeway, Jess remarked, "Let's hope your aunt's not too firm with girls rushing off early for gymnastics."

"You're a gymnast?" Lily Vanessa asked her.

Jess nodded. "Yep . . . and gymnastics starts up again in two weeks. I plan to be in the Olympics someday. How about you? What do you do?"

Lily Vanessa laughed. "I sure don't plan to be in the Olympics! I sing. I sang a solo in my aunt's church on Sunday. Anyhow, that's my talent, except maybe for cooking." No sense in telling them that every time before she sang a solo, she almost died of stage fright.

Tricia said, "Telling about talents is a good way to get to know people fast. My talent is acting, and Becky is very

11

artistic. Cara writes, and Melanie was a New York model. She still models here sometimes, too."

"Wow!" Lily Vanessa said, impressed.

Cat gave another hissy "Pffffittttttttttts!"

"You be good, Cat," Lily Vanessa warned. "I'm trying to find your home for you. I'm trying."

"That cat's a scratcher," Becky remarked.

Lily Vanessa put a finger near Cat, who responded with a swat of a paw and another "Pfffitttttts!"

"I guess she'd scratch me if she could," she remarked. "She doesn't like the cage. It was all I could do to get her in it this morning. You wouldn't think a cat could get so mad."

"Dogs get mad, too," Tricia answered as she took down a yellow poster that had been taped to her breezeway gate.

The poster said,

MORNING FUN FOR KIDS
PLEASE KNOCK ON GATE

Lily Vanessa glanced around as they made their way into the Bennetts' backyard: clay tile water fountain, colorful gym set and sandbox, a tree house in the California pepper tree, and a solid wooden fence around the yard. Craft materials lay all over the redwood picnic table. And a tan cat sunned herself on the pass-through shelf from the kitchen window.

Seeing the other cat, Cat hissed again.

The Bennetts' cat arched her back, ready to fight.

"Ufff!" Tricia said. "I'd better put Butterscotch in the house! Between these two, they'll scare the birds away." She grabbed her cat by the scruff of the neck and rushed her into the house through the sliding glass door. "Come on, Butterscotch. You're not the only cat in the universe."

Lily Vanessa sighed with relief, then looked around the yard again. "This is a really good place for playcare. I heard you do housecleaning and baby-sitting, car washing, and dog-sitting, too. I was wondering if you . . . you know, if you need an extra girl this week. I'm twelve years old and, believe me, I have lots of working experience. I need money for school clothes."

The TCC girls glanced at one another.

Bet they're not sure they want me, Lily Vanessa thought.

"Well," Becky began uneasily, "Tricia, Jess, Cara, and I have known each other for years. When Melanie moved here, the club took her as a trial member. We'd have to get to know you better."

"I can understand that," Lily Vanessa answered. "You don't want some new girl walking in off the street and ruining your club."

Just then, a pretty brown-haired woman opened the kitchen pass-through window. "Well . . . hello!" she said, surprised to see Lily Vanessa.

"Hey, Mom," Tricia said, "this is Lily Vanessa. She's staying at her aunt and uncle's over on La Fortuna this week, but they're working right now. I . . . I invited her for lunch."

"Well, it's nice to meet you, Lily Vanessa." Her green eyes and her smile grew friendly. "I made plenty of hot dogs, so you're especially welcome. Do you go by Lily or Lily Vanessa?"

"All of it. Lily for my great-grandmother from Georgia, who was born on Easter, and Vanessa for my aunt who lives here." She might be tall and skinny and long-footed, but the one thing she liked about herself was her name.

"It's a beautiful name," Mrs. Bennett remarked.

"Thanks. It's different, but I like it, too."

Still smiling, Mrs. Bennett turned to the others. "Hey, guys, clean off the table so you can eat. Hot dogs coming out in a few minutes."

"I'll help," said Lily Vanessa. "What should I do?"

Becky grabbed a blue plastic laundry basket. "All the craft things go in this basket. The rest of you can do clean-up patrol through the yard."

Lily Vanessa helped gather up the craft things while the other girls raced through the yard, picking up mashed graham crackers, empty raisin packs, and paper cups.

"The Funners don't always clean up," Becky explained. "We try to teach them, but they forget. They're only four- to seven-year-olds, and we want them to have fun."

"Sounds like it," Lily Vanessa answered. "I have a little brother and sister myself. They're staying at another aunt's near home this week. I know all about little kids. Ummm, think I'll put Cat and her cage under that tree. Looks like she wants to sleep."

At the kitchen window, Mrs. Bennett passed through a white plastic tablecloth, napkins, flowery paper plates, and real forks and knives. "Here's a dish of cat food for Cat," she said, handing it to Lily Vanessa.

"Thanks. She drank lots of milk and ate a whole can of tuna this morning at my aunt's house. She's been living in the laundry room because my uncle has cat allergies."

Next came people food, and everyone settled at the benches by the table. Lily Vanessa sat between Tricia and

Jess. Becky, Cara, and Melanie sat on the opposite bench.

Hot dogs steamed from the big platter on the table, their spicy smell making Lily Vanessa's mouth water. Bowls held chips, carrot sticks, and apple slices—and there were bottles of ketchup, mustard, and pickle relish. Also glasses of milk.

"Looks good," Lily Vanessa said. She darted a glance at Cat, who was watching them carefully.

"Shall we bow our heads?" Tricia suggested.

Lily Vanessa bowed her head quickly, glad to see that these girls said grace, too.

As they raised their heads, Lily Vanessa added, "Amen!"

They began to pass the hot dogs, and hungry as she was, Lily Vanessa made herself take just one.

"Since you sang at church, I guess you're a Christian, too," Becky remarked to Lily Vanessa.

"I sure am," she answered. "I'm glad to know that you guys are, too!"

Feeling great, Lily Vanessa bit into a hot dog. Ummm . . . the first bite was juicy and delicious. Perfect.

As they ate and talked, she was glad she came. For the last week, she'd only been with her aunt and uncle—and missed her friends at home. She guessed these girls had lots of fun together, and Jess was talking about her upcoming slumber party. Not that Lily Vanessa Shields would be invited!

Mrs. Bennett opened the pass-through window again and handed out the phone.

"Tricia," her mother said, "it's Bear for you."

Tricia thanked her mother, then grabbed the phone. "Hi, Bear. What's happening?"

"Bear's our youth pastor. His real name's Ted Iddings,"

Becky explained to Lily Vanessa across the table. "We just call him Bear. Wonder what's up?"

Everyone quieted, probably listening, too.

"Oh no!" Tricia said. "We forgot it's Youth Sunday."

After a moment, Tricia added, "None of us can sing a solo. Wait . . . you won't believe this, but I do know a singer. She's visiting from L.A., and she's sitting right beside me now. We just met her this morning."

Lily Vanessa straightened her spine uneasily.

She definitely did not want to be dragged into singing again in Santa Rosita. But Ma Darice—her gram—would say, "It's the devil trying to scare you off, girl. He wants you to hold back."

Tricia was saying to the youth minister, "No, I don't know what she sings, but she sang at another church last Sunday. A tape? You'd like to have a tape?"

He must have said "yes" because she turned to Lily Vanessa. "Do you have a tape of your singing?"

"My aunt taped me, but I'm not sure—"

"Yep, she has a tape, Bear," Tricia said. "We'll get a copy of it to you tonight at the youth meeting. We'll try to bring her, too, if we can. Her name's Lily Vanessa Shields, and she's twelve . . . and beautiful."

Beautiful?! Lily Vanessa's brain reeled. *Doesn't she see how tall and skinny and clumsy I am? Doesn't she see my long feet? She didn't even tell him I'm black!*

As for singing, she'd felt all right about it in her L.A. church; after all, Mom's brother—Uncle Isaiah—was the preacher. And Aunt Van's church hadn't been too bad last Sunday . . . but she'd never in her life even dreamed of singing in a mostly white church. No one had said it was all

16

white, but she had a strange feeling. . . .

A shiver of fear raced up her backbone. She'd have stage fright for sure and make a mess of it.

I need your help, Lord, she prayed. *Help me, please!*

CHAPTER

2

*A*t five o'clock, the mouth-watering smell of fried onions and sausage filled the Spanish-style kitchen as Lily Vanessa turned on the oven. She half-wished she hadn't invited the TCCers for dinner. None of them had ever even eaten jambalaya.

What if they don't like it? she thought, then remembered how her invitation had come about.

First, she'd been feeling lonely for friends, and the TCCers seemed like lots of fun. Next, she'd been eating lunch at Tricia's and . . . well, Lily Vanessa's family was always inviting people over for dinner. That was it! It wasn't her fault. The culprit was actually her family's good old-fashioned southern hospitality.

So here she was cooking jambalaya for the Twelve Candles Club girls while they were at Jess's house having their daily four-thirty to five-thirty TCC meeting.

She liked to cook almost as much as she liked to sing and improvise music. Tonight Aunt Van and Uncle Raymond wouldn't be home for dinner, but they'd be pleased to hear she was being hospitable. Hopefully this dinner wouldn't turn out to be the excitement she felt in the air!

She glanced at the small piles of chopped ham, celery, mushrooms, and green peppers on the kitchen counter cutting board. A thought struck, and she belted out like an out-of-control opera singer, "My-O-my, I forgot to steam the rice!" She switched to a rock beat. "Forgot to steam the rice!" Next, she tried "For-uh-got to steam the rice!" to a jazz tempo.

In the pantry, she found a big jar of rice, then hunted for a large measuring container. Back at the white-tile kitchen counter, she started to pour the raw rice into the steamer.

The doorbell rang.

Startled, Lily Vanessa jerked the big glass measuring cup wildly. Rice spilled across the counter and onto the terra-cotta floor—every grain of it!

What a mess!

She tried to scoop the rice on the counter back into the cup. "Coming!" she called out. "I'm coming!" In her rush, her long feet skidded across the rice.

"Yikes!" she yelled, grabbing the kitchen counter to catch her balance. Straightening up, she took a careful step. Rice rolled under her sandals again, flinging her across the floor on one foot like a teetering skater.

The doorbell rang again.

"Coming!!!" Stepping around the biggest pile of rice, she caught her breath. Maybe they'd think it was funny.

As she hurried to the door, a loud *Knock-knock-knock-ety-knock-knock* sounded. Maybe they thought she was pretending not to be home!

Finally she pulled the door open and saw them standing there, but to her amazement, they didn't seem to notice her embarrassment. "Glad you're here!"

Her guests looked slightly uneasy, so she put in, "Come on, that way to the kitchen."

Jess led the way. "This house looks like Cara's . . . and Becky's old house, too. One thing about baby-sitting and cleaning houses, we get to know our way around the different floor plans in Santa Rosita Estates." She turned the corner toward the kitchen counter.

Too late, Lily Vanessa warned, "Watch out for the rice!"

"Yikes!" Jess shouted as she skidded.

Cara followed, yelling and flailing her arms until she caught herself on the kitchen counter.

To make them feel better, Lily Vanessa slid in across the rice with them, arms out wide. "Look at me skate!" she announced. "I could be an Olympic rice skater!" Cara, Tricia, and Melanie slid in behind her, laughing, and before long they were all leaning on the kitchen counters, shaking with laughter.

"We must be the champion rice skaters of the world!" Tricia declared.

They laughed so hard that Lily Vanessa's eyes filled with tears. What a way to make friends!

When they finally calmed down, Lily Vanessa and Cara started hiccuping, bringing on another bout of hysterics.

"Stop it, guys!" Melanie begged. "My side hurts!"

Finally they sat on the floor in the midst of the rice. "A

21

good thing Aunt Van has lots of rice," Lily Vanessa said. "We're sure not eating skated-on rice for dinner."

She pulled the wastebasket from under the kitchen sink, and they scooped rice into piles with their hands, then dumped it into the trash. Luckily, everyone seemed to be having a great time at it.

Tricia asked, "Why do you have Cat out on the sidewalk in her cage?"

Lily Vanessa dumped the last handful of rice, then put the wastebasket back under the sink. "I was hoping the owners might see her. Besides, my uncle has cat allergies."

They got up from the floor, standing out of her way, and she poured another three cups of rice into the steamer, then added the water.

"What if someone steals her?" Cara asked.

Lily Vanessa turned on the steamer. "I don't think anyone would since you said there are always lots of strays around. One thing's sure. Aunt Van and Uncle Raymond can't keep Cat here."

"I have an idea," Cara said, her brown eyes dancing.

"Believe me, I'm all ears!" Lily Vanessa told her.

Everyone looked at Cara, and she turned a little shy. "I was thinking of Cat Woman—the old lady who lives by the canyon at the south end of this street. Actually, her land meets the south end of all of Santa Rosita Estates. People say she has millions of cats. Maybe Cat belongs to her."

"Maybe," Jess said. "But she's spooky—really spooky. Last week, Mom went over there to see if Cat Woman wanted to list her property for sale. She owns ten acres down in the canyon. Also a run-down house and other tumble-down buildings hidden in that jungle of trees and vines

. . . not to mention an army of cats, some dogs, and a two-hundred-and-fifty-pound goat."

Tricia explained to Lily Vanessa, "Jess's mom's a realtor."

"Did anything happen to your mom?" Cara asked.

Jess lifted her hands. "Cat Woman ran at her, yelling for her to get out of there. Mom said she backed the Jeep out fast, down her very long driveway, all the way to the street."

"We could sneak over and ask if Cat belongs to her—"

"No way," Jess replied. "She's got 'no trespassing' signs stuck all over, and from what Mom says, we don't want to get involved with Cat Woman."

"Maybe we could try to leave Cat near there," Lily Vanessa said. "Just *near* there. If she belongs to Cat Woman, she'd probably stay."

"You'd think so," Cara replied.

Lily Vanessa dumped the meat, vegetables, and tomato paste into a big casserole dish, then stirred it all up with a big wooden spoon. They were still discussing how to leave Cat when she stuck the casserole into the oven. "Let's go! The oven's set to turn off in an hour, and I have the front door key."

On the way out, she locked the front door, grabbed Cat and her cage, and followed the TCCers. Yep, it'd be best to drop Cat off at Cat Woman's place. So far, that seemed to be the only answer.

They walked along the sidewalk toward the edge of Santa Rosita Estates. After a while, it was peculiar to see the development houses end and an old, run-down place begin with a tangle of shrubbery and towering eucalyptus trees.

"How come your mom wants to get Cat Woman to sell the property?" Tricia asked.

Jess shrugged. "Mom says our developer—you know, the Santa Rosita Estates builder—wants to add more houses on this side of the development. If they did, you could drive straight through to Hill Road."

Tricia said, "So it'd be a faster way to drive around. And the developer would make money on the houses, too."

"Yeah," Jess answered.

As they approached the battered white horse fence, Lily Vanessa eyed Cat Woman's land. Huge eucalyptus trees grew from steep canyons and smaller ravines, surrounded by bushes and tall grasses. "They'd have to bulldoze it all down flat to build houses."

"Looks like it," Cara agreed. "I'd hate to see more houses here. It's the only place near Santa Rosita Estates that's still wild, even if everything does look run down."

The others agreed, and Cat let out a loud, "Meowww!"

"Shhhh!" Lily Vanessa warned her. "We don't want any dogs chasing us. You'll have plenty of cat company soon."

"Guess we'll have to climb the fence," Jess said.

The white wooden fence wasn't much of a challenge, Lily Vanessa decided as they began to climb over it. Old rose bushes trailed around the fence, most of them dead, but the stems still had thorns.

Once over the splintery fence, Lily Vanessa and the others struggled through the overgrown bushes for a long, long while, then arrived at a wire fence.

"The property is double-fenced!" Jess exclaimed.

"Well, let's go through," Tricia said. "That's the only way to find out where the cats are."

They held the wires apart for each other and slipped through, one after another.

Beyond the fence, the trees, grasses, and bushes were neatly trimmed back like a park. Strange, such a sudden change of scenery—from a wild tangle to a neat park.

Nearby, a hand-lettered sign said, "WATCH OUT FOR GOAT."

"Watch out for goat?" Lily Vanessa asked.

Becky shook her head. "If there's a goat here, we'd better watch out, all right. I hear they'll eat anything. Even clothes off a clothesline."

"You think the goat ate the bushes and grass here?" Lily Vanessa asked.

"Come to think of it," Jess said, "Mom might have mentioned that, too. Next time I'll pay more attention."

In the distance, a dog began to bark. Before long, two or three other dogs joined in.

Lily Vanessa stopped with the others.

"It's okay," Jess said. "Mom said the dogs are chained to poles near the house and the stable. They're mean dogs—watch dogs. And we'd better watch out for snakes."

"Snakes?!" Lily Vanessa echoed. She never saw snakes where she lived. Just then, she walked under a tree and into a spider web. "A-i-i-i!" she wailed, wiping it off wildly.

"There're rattlesnakes around here," Jess said. "Come on, let's go this way. The house is somewhere in the middle of the property. We need to find the driveway."

Slowly they made their way along, nervously watching for snakes; instead, they found gopher holes. Careful not to step into them, they climbed from the shallow gullies into steeper ravines, and then back to flatter land again. Even with the bushes and trees trimmed, the unevenness of the land put treetops at different levels, making it hard to see far ahead.

Some distance farther, a beat-up red pickup truck stood in a gully. As they neared the truck, they saw it had no tires and was standing on blocks. The doors hung open, their windows broken.

Cat meowed, but not too loudly.

Lily Vanessa tried to soothe her. "Almost there, even if we don't see any cats so far."

"Look out!" Becky called out, pointing. "There's the goat behind the truck! Wow . . . he's huge . . . and he has horns and a beard!"

The white goat must have seen them at that moment, too, because his ears perked up.

"It must be the watch-out-for-goat goat!" Cara said. "Come on! Let's get out of here!"

The goat eyed them drowsily, then began to amble in their direction, moving faster and faster. As he neared them he lowered his head and let out a deep, warning "Meaaaaah!"

"Here he comes!" Jess shouted. "Run! Run!"

They raced wildly, tripping over roots, but never quite falling.

Lily Vanessa glanced back. "He's gaining on us!"

At long last, she saw the wire fence ahead of them and decided that this must be "the excitement" she'd expected.

Breathless, she ignored Cat's arched back and hisses. She pushed the cage through the wires, then clambered through the fence herself.

On the other side, she grabbed Cat's cage again. Turning back, she saw the goat still running at them full speed. "Here he comes!"

They raced through the overgrown weeds and bushes. "Run!" Becky yelled.

"What if he follows us home?!" Melanie called out.

When Lily Vanessa glanced back, she could scarcely believe her eyes. She slowed her long feet. "The goat stopped by that puny wire fence. He just stopped."

The TCCers turned and stopped themselves.

"I can't believe it," Tricia said.

"Why do you think he stopped?" Lily Vanessa asked as she tried to catch her breath.

The TCCers stood with her, as surprised as she was to see the goat standing behind the fence, staring at them with drowsy-eyed interest.

"Maybe he's trained to stop at the fence," Cara guessed. "Maybe it used to be an electric fence, and he got shocked."

"That's hard to believe," Jess argued.

"It could be, though," Becky said. "Just look at him standing there."

They decided that had to be it. Somehow the goat believed he couldn't get through the fence.

After a while, he began to lose interest in them. Finally he turned his hindquarters to them and slowly picked his way back deeper into the property.

Still watching, they brushed dirt and small twigs off their clothing.

"Strange goat," Melanie said. "I thought he'd chase us all the way home."

"Me too," Jess agreed.

"Maybe he's an old goat," Lily Vanessa put in. "Maybe he can't see very well."

"Maybe," Cara said. "Who knows? Maybe he's been eating that old red truck!"

They all laughed, but Cat gave a fierce "Meowww!!!"

"Sorry, Cat," Lily Vanessa said, "we forgot all about you. Guess you'll have to come back home for now."

"Later, we could go back with Cat and go in around from another side," Jess suggested.

No way! Lily Vanessa thought at first.

"Anyhow, it was an adventure," Tricia said. "The kind we probably won't forget."

Lily Vanessa shook her head, tumbling her corn-row braids. "You guys, I'm not used to living so close to the wilderness! I'm not used to this kind of adventure!"

"Actually, we're not either," Cara answered.

"I've got a feeling," Lily Vanessa answered. "A bad feeling that Cat really belongs there and that we'll have to bring her back again."

CHAPTER

3

When they returned to Aunt Van's house, it was just six-thirty and the sun still shone brightly—one of the things Lily Vanessa liked best about summer. She opened the front door, and the aroma of jambalaya made her mouth water.

"Ummmmm . . . it smells good," Jess said.

"It ought to be done now for sure. The onions and sausage were already cooked," Lily Vanessa told them. "Baking it all together blends in the tomato paste with the ham and sausage flavors. I also have a salad cooling in the refrigerator."

Cara remarked, "You must really like cooking."

"Almost as much as singing," Lily Vanessa laughed.

As they made their way into the kitchen, Tricia suggested, "We could set the table for you."

"Thanks, I'll take Cat to the laundry room first." Eyeing the floor for rice, Lily Vanessa added, "No more rice on the floor for skating."

They laughed with her.

In the laundry room, she opened the cage and Cat leapt out. "Cool it, Cat. Here's some nice tuna and water for you." Cat headed straight for the tuna.

"I do believe you're fatter since you've been here," Lily Vanessa remarked, but Cat was too occupied with eating to notice. "Don't even purr then, you ungrateful cat!"

When Lily Vanessa returned to the kitchen, she took out six placemats, glasses, napkins, and white dishes, and set them by the side counter. "Silverware's in that drawer. We'll use the dining area table."

The small dining area was an L-shaped space off the living room, perfect for Aunt Van and Uncle Raymond since they didn't have children. Six light oak chairs stood around a matching table, which was topped by a red silk amaryllis centerpiece. An antique brass chandelier hung over the table, and a large picture of an ancient church decorated the buffet wall.

"Hey, I like these placemats," Becky remarked as she began to set them out. "Look at the paintings on them." She read their descriptions from small print in the lower corners. "York Church and City Wall . . . Bridge in Yorkshire . . . Fountains Abbey, Yorkshire . . . Whitby Harbour, Yorkshire . . . The Bronte Parsonage . . ."

"Only our artist, Becky, would notice," Jess said.

"My aunt and uncle got them in England," Lily Vanessa explained. "When they travel, they buy stuff for the house. That picture on the wall is from England, too." She liked the large picture of ancient church ruins, herself. "We're always getting ourselves more educated. There're lots of teachers in my family."

"Think you'll be one?" Melanie asked.

Lily Vanessa shrugged. "Maybe. There aren't many good jobs for singers, and I don't think I'd want to spend my whole life cooking, either."

Before long, the table was set, and Lily Vanessa found a big metal trivet for under the hot casserole. "Table looks nice. I'll get the jambalaya."

The TCCers served the salads and stacked the dinner plates by Lily Vanessa's placemat. She carried in the casserole. The steaming jambalaya gave off a heavenly aroma. Mom always claimed a cook couldn't go wrong serving jambalaya.

In the dining area, she put it on the trivet near her placemat. "I'll serve from here. Go ahead, sit down."

They sat, then looked at her expectantly.

"Prayer! I was so busy, I nearly forgot about the Lord!" They bowed their heads, and Lily Vanessa said, "Thanks for this day . . . even for the rice fiasco and the goat chase . . . and now for this food." She thought about thanking Him for these new friends, then decided to wait to see how that turned out. She quickly added, "In Jesus' name we pray. Amen."

When they raised their heads, Tricia said, "I guess God must have laughed about the rice fiasco and goat chase, too. We must have looked funny."

Lily Vanessa smiled at the thought and began to ladle jambalaya onto the plates. "If God's got a sense of humor like my Uncle Isaiah claims, He must have been laughing like mad."

It occurred to her that it felt comfortable to have these girls here. Last week, if someone had told her about the goat chase and this dinner, she'd have thought they were crazy.

Jess asked, "What are we going to do about Cat?"

"Go back to Cat Woman's after dinner?" Lily Vanessa questioned.

Jess said, "I don't see any other way."

"Yikes!" Tricia interrupted. "We have youth group practice tonight for Sunday's program. We're rehearsing the whole program. Can you come with us?"

Lily Vanessa shrugged. She didn't want to ask the question that came to mind, then asked it anyhow. "Will I be the only black person there?"

Tricia nodded. "Probably. But that's no big deal."

"I go there," Melanie said, "and I'm ABC . . . you know, American-born Chinese. Cara usually comes, too—"

"And I'm half Hispanic," Cara explained. "People are nice in that church. It's okay to be different there."

Finished serving the jambalaya, Lily Vanessa sat down. "Let me think about going tonight."

Tricia smiled, her green eyes dancing. "You'll have lots of fun if you do."

The others nodded.

"Hey," Becky said to Lily Vanessa, "we forgot to ask. If you want to work, we could use help tomorrow morning washing cars. Everyone wants their cars washed, and only Tricia and I are available."

"Thanks, I'd like to do that," Lily Vanessa told them.

"Good, that makes three of us," Becky said.

"Glad to help," Lily Vanessa answered. She forked up some jambalaya. Ummm . . . the rice was done and so were the chopped celery and peppers and the rest of it.

"This is great!" Jess declared.

The others were equally impressed.

"Maybe you could teach cooking on television," Becky said. "I can already see it in the TV pages. *Lily Vanessa's Southern Cooking.* 'Today Lily Vanessa is teaching us how to make jambalaya . . . and how to outrun a gigantic goat while the casserole's cooking in the oven.' "

Lily Vanessa let out a loud *Ha!* "I hadn't thought about teaching cooking. But I guess there're all kinds of teaching jobs, when you think about it."

She was dishing up seconds to the TCCers when the doorbell rang. "Wonder who that could be. Back in a minute."

When she opened the door, her grandmother stood beaming at her and wearing a brown-and-white African-style fabric dress over her ample body. "Surprise!"

"Ma Darice! I thought you were still in Africa—"

"Came home early," Ma Darice replied in her low musical voice. She set a white bakery box and a big shopping bag on the entry table, and threw her arms around Lily Vanessa. "Just wait till you hear about Africa. I rented a video camera, and one of these days we'll have a family show."

It sounded interesting, but Lily Vanessa thought that right now she'd rather be in Ma Darice's arms for a long time. "I'm glad you're home."

Her grandmother laughed. "I do feel welcomed. Actually, I had a meeting in San Diego today, and I heard you were here with Van and Raymond. Thought I'd try to lay over till freeway traffic thins down . . . if I'm welcome."

"You're welcome for sure," Lily Vanessa answered.

Ma Darice sniffed the air. "Ummm, it smells good in here. Jambalaya?"

Lily Vanessa laughed. "It is. I made it."

"You made it? You made it all yourself?"

"I did, just the way you always told me."

"Shouldn't be surprised, but I'm still impressed," her grandmother said. "I picked up an apple pie for dessert." She gave her the white bakery box from the entry table.

"Perfect," Lily Vanessa answered. "I was going to serve the vanilla ice cream from the freezer."

"Together that makes apple pie á la mode."

"It does!"

Ma Darice looked toward the TCCers talking in the dining area. "You've got somebody else visiting—"

"New friends," Lily Vanessa said. "I think you'd like to meet them. They have a working club and jobs all over the neighborhood."

"Sounds interesting," Ma Darice replied. "I'll just leave the shopping bag here for now."

"What's in it?"

Ma Darice laughed in her low musical voice. "Show you in a while."

In the dining room, Lily Vanessa saw the TCCers eye her grandmother. "Girls," she began, "this is my grandmother, Mrs. Darice Williams."

"This is Cara and Jess and . . ."

As Lily Vanessa introduced them, she watched Ma Darice take an interest in each of them. Not that there was anything new about that; Ma Darice always took an interest in people.

"You gals can call me Ma Darice, too," she told them. "I just returned from a visit to Africa, and they greeted me there with, 'Jambo, Mama.' Made me sound like a jumbo-sized mama. It's a relief to be back to Ma Darice again."

The TCCers laughed with her.

"Let me get you some salad and jambalaya," Lily Vanessa offered. "You can sit in my chair. I'll get a folding chair."

"Talked me right into dinner," Ma Darice said with a chuckle. "Didn't take much talking, either, did it?"

The TCCers smiled and seemed interested in her.

When Lily Vanessa returned with a folding chair, they'd already made room for another place at the table and were enjoying one another's company.

"Tricia said you're singing at her church," Ma Darice said.

Lily Vanessa shrugged. "Maybe. The youth minister hasn't heard my tape yet."

Her grandmother smiled proudly. "Unless he has a tin ear, you'll be singing. That much I know."

She turned to the TCCers. "My granddaughter has a voice like an angel's."

"Ma Darice is the real singer in the family," Lily Vanessa told them. "When my gramp was alive, he always said being around her was like living in a gospel concert."

"We do have a singing family," Ma Darice replied with a laugh. "It's a hard career, though, being a singer. We don't want Lily Vanessa to be just another singer chasing around the country on a bus like most singers do. It's a hard life . . . even harder if you're married and have children."

Lily Vanessa tended to agree, mainly because she always had such bad stage fright. Besides, there were thousands of really good singers. As for being married and having a family, that seemed hundreds of years away.

Ma Darice smiled at her. "I'll be in church Sunday to pray you through the notes. I wouldn't miss it for anything."

Lily Vanessa beamed. With her grandmother there praying, it'd be easier. Just having her come for dinner had turned the meal into a real party.

By the time everyone helped themselves to apple pie, Ma Darice knew all about Cat and Cat Woman and the goat chase, too.

"It's a story to remember," she told them, her brown eyes sparkling. "Now who wants to hear a little about my trip to Africa, the land of Lily Vanessa's and my ancestors?"

Everyone did.

Ma Darice pushed her chair back from the table. "First of all, the trip wasn't perfect. But in some places, it was surprising and wonderful."

She raised her brows thoughtfully. "Now what shall I tell? Ummmm . . . yes. About the day our zebra-striped minivans parked way above the famous Ngorongoro Crater, which has lions and antelope . . . all kinds of what we might call zoo animals. . . .

"Well, we tourists settled on nearby rocks to enjoy our box lunches when we saw a Masai herdsman watching his cattle graze on a nearby hillside. He was thin, almost bony, standing on the hill with his wooden staff and a big gourd—a calabash—slung over his shoulder like someone from a travel poster.

"I said to the others, 'I'm going to see if that man and I can have a conversation.' Everyone laughed and said, 'Yeah, yeah, Darice. All you know in Masai is *Jambo, Mama.*'"

The TCCers smiled, and Ma Darice continued.

"I climbed up that hillside and called out 'Jambo' to

him. He turned around slowly and, with a very British accent, said, 'Good day, madam. Are you enjoying your journey through my country?' "

She smiled. "I was so surprised, I couldn't answer for a moment. Finally I asked how he happened to speak English. It turned out that he'd attended Oxford University in England, one of the best universities in the world.

" 'And you left there?' I asked him.

"The Masai man nodded. 'I found I prefer herding cattle on the hills of Africa to the so-called civilized life,' he told me."

"You're kidding!" Lily Vanessa said.

Ma Darice shook her head.

"Words failed me," she told them. "For once, words failed me. Luckily, the minivan driver honked the horn for me to join them, and I told the Masai man it was interesting to have heard his story."

No one spoke, then Lily Vanessa asked, "That's it?"

Ma Darice nodded. "That's it. He had a chance others can only dream of, but he gave it up to live as a cattle herder where he felt he was called to be."

Everyone quietly sat around the dining table.

"An interesting story, isn't it?" asked Ma Darice. "Almost like one of Jesus' parables. A person samples the world on a platter, but he finally sees what's most important."

Jess asked her, "What do you think is important?"

Ma Darice drew another long breath. "The way I see it, it's loving God and your neighbor as yourself."

Tricia remarked, "Like it says in the Bible."

Ma Darice nodded. "Yes, like it says in the Bible. And you know what? I met a lot of people in Africa who were

Christians. It was wonderful."

She waited for a while, then smiled broadly. "Now if you ladies will clear this table, I've brought Lily Vanessa and her family some presents from Africa. I think I might just have something for the rest of you, too."

Lily Vanessa felt her lips edge up in a smile, and she made the rest of her jump up to clear the table.

Ma Darice said, "I'll just get that shopping bag I left in the front entry."

When they all settled at the table again, Ma Darice lifted the white tissue paper from the top of the shopping bag. "First, here's one of my presents to me."

She lifted a long reddish brown gourd with a leather strap from the bag. "A calabash, just like that Masai herdsman had over his shoulder. Smell inside. You'll probably think it smells like salami."

They passed the gourd around the table, everyone lifting off the pointed lid.

"It smells like salami, all right," Lily Vanessa said. "Ufff! It's terrible."

Ma Darice laughed. "Actually, it's the smell of cattle blood. They drain the blood from their cattle and mix it with milk for drinking."

"O-o-oh gross!" Lily Vanessa exclaimed with disgust.

"Gross!" the TCCers agreed.

Ma Darice laughed again. "It's not my way or your way, but it's the Masai way. And you know what? I didn't see a fat person like me among them."

She dug in the shopping bag and brought out two small wooden carvings of Masai people for Aunt Van and Uncle Raymond. "To stand on their coffee table," she decided.

"And here's a small drum covered with brown-and-white cattle hide I brought back for a musician friend."

Finally she pulled out a small box. "Now here's my present for Lily Vanessa."

"Is it gross, too?"

Ma Darice shook her head. "Nothing gross for you, my dear."

Lily Vanessa opened the box slowly. "A bracelet!" A gold-colored metal one to slip over her wrist. "A bracelet from Africa!"

"Yes," Ma Darice said, "a brass bracelet from Africa, from the land of your ancestors."

An important bracelet, Lily Vanessa thought as she thanked her grandmother.

Ma Darice brought out tiny carved animals barely bigger than charms. "I brought back lots for a class at your mother's school. I promised I'd tell them about Africa when school starts. Here, you each pick one out."

The TCCers thanked her and admired the tiny carvings of lions, leopards, and rhinoceros.

"You should have seen the real animals," Ma Darice said.

Lily Vanessa asked, "Which did you like best?"

"The elephants. I wish everyone could see a herd of them crossing a river, the mother elephants spraying water over their babies. It's a sight I'll never forget."

"Someday I want to go to Africa," Lily Vanessa decided.

Suddenly Tricia looked at her watch. "Yipes! It's time for the youth group meeting. Mom will be waiting to take us!" She turned to Lily Vanessa. "Can you go?"

Lily Vanessa drew a breath. "I'd like to stay here with

Ma Darice. But I'll get you the tape now."

Moments later, Tricia had the tape and the TCCers rushed out the door. "See you tomorrow morning to wash cars," they called back. "Eight o'clock at Tricia's house."

"Eight o'clock!" Lily Vanessa answered. " 'Bye!"

She turned to Ma Darice. "I'm hoping maybe one of their customers is the owner of Cat!"

"Maybe," Ma Darice said. "It wouldn't surprise me."

Lily Vanessa hoped so. It'd be a lot better than sneaking back to Cat Woman's house tomorrow.

CHAPTER

4

*T*he next morning—Thursday—Lily Vanessa hummed happily as she headed down the sidewalk carrying Cat, who not surprisingly hissed in her cage.

"After everything I've done for you, the least I'd expect from you is one small purr," she told Cat firmly. "Or don't you know how?"

Cat only arched her back and spat furiously.

"No sense of gratitude," Lily Vanessa said. "I'll bet you're not even a house cat. Probably a wild cat!"

The morning sun slanted down through the trees, and birds sang from the leafy branches, cheering her in spite of Cat's bad manners. After a while, her thoughts wandered back to last night after the TCCers had left. She felt glad Ma Darice had liked them a lot, just as they'd liked her.

She hoped she'd be a strong and loving woman like her grandmother someday. Of course, Ma Darice claimed her strength came from the Lord. She was the one with the strongest faith of everyone in the family except, of course, Uncle Isaiah. A good preacher had to have strong faith. Mom and Dad probably had just as much faith in their jobs as Ma Darice did in God.

A dog barked, interrupting Lily Vanessa's train of thought. Cat swung around in the cage toward the barking and hissed again.

"Calm down, Cat," Lily Vanessa told her. "We're going to Tricia's house. It's car-washing morning. If you're not careful, we'll wash you."

A car coming from the other direction pulled into Tricia's driveway. Looked like it was Becky and her new stepfather dropping her off. Yep, Becky got out, two plastic buckets in hand, and slammed the car door.

As the car backed out, Lily Vanessa waved. "Hey, Becky!"

Becky turned, smiled, and waved back.

Just then Tricia came out her breezeway gate carrying plastic shopping bags and buckets. "Thank goodness you're here!" she exclaimed, seeing them. "I was beginning to think I'd have to do all of the car washing."

Lily Vanessa rushed along to Tricia's driveway and, once there, peered into the buckets. Sponges, squeegees, soap pads, plastic bottles of liquid soap, and blue window-washing stuff. "How many cars do we wash?"

"Seven this morning," Tricia answered. "Not to mention three minivans."

Becky laughed like someone who was used to washing lots of cars. "Just so it's not *moving* vans."

"No way!" Lily Vanessa chimed in, laughing herself.

"Grab some bags and buckets," Tricia said. "We begin at the Hutchinsons'. They were our first car-washing customers. Usually we wash their cars on Saturdays, but they're having a last camping trip before school starts, so they've switched this week to Thursday."

Lily Vanessa grabbed two bags by the handles and headed up the sidewalk. "We must look funny walking along with bags, buckets, and all of this stuff. Not to mention me carrying a cage with a wild cat in it."

"I've looked funnier, believe me," Becky answered. "In fact, this has to be our wildest summer ever, and we've lived next door to each other since our playpen days."

They walked along in silence for a while.

"How'd the youth meeting go last night?" Lily Vanessa asked. "Did your youth pastor want me to sing?"

"He didn't have a chance to listen to the tape, but you're the one and only—and the very best—candidate we have for a solo," Tricia answered.

That made it sound as if she'd be singing, Lily Vanessa thought. She still wasn't sure how she felt about that.

The Hutchinsons' old white Honda and new green minivan were parked on the driveway by their pale yellow two-story house. A large coil of garden hose lay in the grass near the driveway.

Lily Vanessa plopped the cage in the shade of the garage. "Here you are, Cat. Now stop your complaining."

That done, she glanced at Becky and Tricia uneasily. "Ummmm. . . . I've got something to confess. I was going to mention it last night, but everyone was talking and then Ma Darice came."

"What's that?" Becky asked.

n't have any car-washing experience—Mom always
car washed at a place near school."

"It's easy," Tricia assured her. "Just hose off the car, wash it with sudsy water, scrub the wheels, bumpers, and tires, then rinse with the hose and wipe the car dry. Last, spray the windows with the blue window-washing stuff and dry them with the paper towels."

"Piece of cake," Lily Vanessa said, relieved. Becky was already filling two buckets with sudsy water, and Tricia hosed off the cars.

"Ready for the soap!" Tricia called out.

Lily Vanessa grabbed a big sponge and soaped up the Honda. "Looks like you guys have the job all figured out."

She was spraying the Honda's windows when Mrs. Hutchinson came out with a letter to put in her mailbox. "Good morning, girls. Isn't it a beautiful morning?"

They returned her greeting and Becky added, "It is. Oh, this is Lily Vanessa Shields, who's helping us today."

"It's a pleasure to meet you," Mrs. Hutchinson replied.

"Hi," Lily Vanessa said, feeling oddly shy.

Suddenly she remembered and nodded toward the cat cage. "Do you happen to know who that cat belongs to?"

Mrs. Hutchinson looked at Cat. "Never saw her before."

Lily Vanessa asked a hopeful, "Do you by chance want a beautiful cat?"

"No thanks," the woman said. "We already have a cat and a dog. No more pets. Maybe another client will want her."

"That's what I'm hoping," Lily Vanessa answered.

When they finished at the Hutchinsons, the car and minivan gleamed. Even better, when Mrs. Hutchinson came out to pay them, she remarked, "Good job, as usual. I hope you girls will have time for car washing once you're back in school."

"We hope to," Becky told her. "We like to work together."

"So I notice," Mrs. Hutchinson replied with a smile. She turned to Lily Vanessa, the smile replaced with regret. "Sorry we can't take another cat."

"Somebody else might," Lily Vanessa answered.

But at the next house, they didn't want a cat either. Nor did the people at the next, nor the next, nor after that.

"I guess you're just not wanted, Cat," Lily Vanessa told her sadly. "I don't know . . . even with your bad attitude, there's something special about you. We just don't know what it is yet."

Cat turned around and around in her cage, ignoring her. "If we take her to Cat Woman's, cat won't be lonely for other pets," Lily Vanessa said to the others. "Maybe that's what we're supposed to do."

By one o'clock, the car and minivan washing was finished, but she still had Cat to carry home with her.

As they walked along, the buckets full of wet rags, Lily Vanessa noticed that her brass African bracelet was shinier. Probably from the soap and window-washing solution. The bracelet shone brightly in the sunshine, lifting her spirits. *Africa.* She tried to imagine what it'd be like living there in the "bush," which is what people called the wilderness there. Interesting maybe, but no way would she want to live there!

After a while she asked, "Can you guys stop at my house

for peanut butter and jelly sandwiches, then maybe we can take Cat to Cat Woman's?"

Becky shrugged. "I'm here for the rest of the day with Tricia. The TCC meeting at Jess's isn't until four-thirty."

"I'll call home and ask," Tricia said.

"Me too," Becky added. "Are you sure your aunt doesn't mind us eating at her house again?"

"No way," Lily Vanessa assured them. "She was glad you'd all been there for dinner last night. She feels guilty leaving me here alone while she's at meetings."

Fifteen minutes later, they sat at her aunt's kitchen counter making sandwiches. The counter held bread, peanut butter, jelly, pickles, chips, milk, lemonade, grapes, and apples.

"Too bad you don't live here all the time," Becky said to Lily Vanessa. "We'd have a lot of fun together."

"You bet we would," Tricia added.

Lily Vanessa smiled and spread peanut butter across a slice of toasted bread. "Thanks. You probably think so because since that goat chase, it hasn't been dull here."

"That's for sure, it hasn't been dull!" Becky answered with a laugh. "But I think I'd like you anyhow."

"Thanks!" Lily Vanessa lined up pickle slices on top of her peanut buttered slice of bread. She thought they'd react to her peculiar sandwich, but they just eyed her oddly and didn't say anything. "It hasn't been dull for me, either," she told them, "not since I met you guys."

"It's been an all-around interesting summer," Tricia said, "even before going to Cat Woman's place."

"Let's figure out a better way to leave Cat there this time," Lily Vanessa suggested. "Maybe go in from the roadside. Then if the goat appears, one of us could distract it while the other two deliver Cat."

"Great idea," Tricia said. "I volunteer to distract the goat. It'd be good acting experience if I ever have to act in a bullfight scene."

"A bullfight?!" Becky asked. "Come on, you wacko!"

Tricia pressed her lips together, trying not to laugh with her mouth full. Finally she swallowed. "I should have a red cape. A good-sized red cape for waving at that goat—"

"How about a red tablecloth?" Lily Vanessa suggested. "Aunt Van has some small red tablecloths for card tables."

Becky laughed. "I can't believe what I'm hearing! And just when Cara isn't around to video-tape it! This is the kind of scene—waving off a goat with a red tablecloth—that would get us all movie jobs!"

Laughing, Lily Vanessa hopped down from the counter stool and headed for the tablecloth cabinet. "You know what? If it weren't for Cat, I'd never have met you guys. I guess I should be giving thanks for that cat."

It occurred to her that there might be something even more special about Cat. Something they hadn't realized yet, but something. . . .

What was it?

The "excitement" she felt sure was coming?

———————

At two o'clock they started out for Cat Woman's again. This time, though, when they left Santa Rosita Estates behind, they turned left by the Cat Woman's battered white fence. Lily Vanessa carried the red tablecloth while Tricia and Becky led the way since they knew the neighborhood.

They stayed outside the fence in the dried weeds and bushes, sometimes detouring for huge eucalyptus trees. Keeping an eye out for snakes and gopher holes, they went on for a longer way from this direction.

Lily Vanessa carried Cat's cage away from her side since, as usual, Cat was mad. It was bad enough having to put up with Cat's terrible manners without worrying about what might leap out at her from the bushes and trees. She'd no more than thought it than she walked right into a huge spider web. "Yuck!"

"Spider web?" Tricia asked.

"Uh-huh." Lily Vanessa shuddered as she wiped it off. "I walked into one, too."

They were quiet for a while, then Tricia whispered, "No sign of the goat yet!"

"Thank goodness!" Becky whispered back. "We must be halfway to the other side of the property by now. I suppose we could have gone to the driveway instead of climbing the fence, but we'd be caught for sure."

"Come on," Tricia said.

They climbed over the white fence and slowly ventured onto Cat Woman's place. Once they were well into the wild tangle of plants, they peered in more deeply. There was the same kind of double strand wire fence some distance away. Beyond it, all of the shrubs and trees were trimmed off high there too.

"Hey, there's an old road ahead!" Tricia told them. "I'll bet that rusted old truck was at the end of the road. We must have curved back somehow. Let's go in here."

Finally the overgrown shrubbery was behind them. They held the wire fence apart for one another and climbed through into the parklike area.

Here and there, chicken wire surrounded clumps of bushes, probably for protection. Slowly, they made their way toward the old road. Once on it, they found gray gravel in the tire ruts and pot holes as if someone had tried to fill them years ago.

Tricia whispered, "We'd better stay off the gravel places. It might crunch under our feet."

They tiptoed along in the dirt.

After a while Becky whispered, "Look at those buildings ahead. Everything needs paint. It's sure run down."

Lily Vanessa held Cat's cage to the side. She was used to the city and suburbs and their parks, but nothing like this strange place. It seemed even spookier than it had yesterday.

As they curved around through the trees, another "WATCH OUT FOR GOAT" sign stood alongside the path.

Tricia unfolded the small red tablecloth. The plan was for her to head over to the side where the goat was last night and hold him off, while Becky and Lily Vanessa found the cats and decided if Cat felt at home here.

Far up the driveway, a dog barked.

Another barked with him.

Startled, the girls came to a dead stop.

Finally the dogs quieted.

"Go on," Tricia whispered. "I'll head for the goat's place now. I think the rusty truck is up that path."

Lily Vanessa waved Tricia on. Her arm caught in the bare twigs of a nearby bush and she twisted it out. Just a scratch mark. No blood. "Uff!"

"You okay?" Becky asked.

Lily Vanessa nodded. "I'm okay."

They watched while Tricia made her way up the side path, angling into a nearby gully.

After a while Becky whispered, "Here come the cats!"

Cats slowly padded from behind one of the clumps of bushes surrounded with chicken wire. First three cats, then two more, then more and more until they were circled by a ghostly horde of silent cats. Cat watched them and purred contentedly.

Now! Lily Vanessa told herself. *Now is the time to let Cat out!*

The cats watched her as she set the cage down and opened it. "Go on, Cat," she whispered. "This seems like your home to me. Look at all of your friends. Get out."

Cat purred again. But instead of leaving the cage, she hunched against the back of it.

"Go on, Cat! Go on!"

But Cat was not about to get out of the cage.

"Push her," Becky said.

Next, Lily Vanessa tried to ease Cat out. No use.

Finally she tipped the cage and gave Cat a firm push.

"Meowwwwwwww!" Cat complained loudly.

Other cats meowed back.

Suddenly dogs barked, and from the distance, Tricia came running and yelling, "Run, guys, run for Hill Road! Here comes that goat!"

Becky and Lily Vanessa turned and ran up the driveway. When they glanced back, Tricia had stopped and waved the red tablecloth at the goat, but it only stopped him for a moment.

His horns gleamed wickedly, and he ran as if he planned to attack.

"Run, Tricia!" Becky yelled. "Run!"

Tricia flapped the red tablecloth at the goat again, then took off running to the old road. "Don't wait for me!"

Becky and Lily Vanessa ran on ahead, and Tricia began to catch up.

They heard the goat's hooves pounding on the dirt road behind them, and they ran on with all of their might.

In the distance, a woman yelled, "Quiet, you dogs! Come here, Brutus!"

Brutus!? Lily Vanessa thought.

When she looked back through the trees, no one was in sight, but the goat had slowed. Now he came to a stop.

They ran on anyhow, huffing and puffing.

Behind them, Tricia gasped, "I just remembered, it's red capes and movement that *attract* bulls! . . . It doesn't scare them off! Must be the same with goats."

They were still huffing and puffing when they finally reached Hill Road, "Let's hope Cat is happy back there," Becky said.

"After all we've done for that cat, let's hope so!" Lily Vanessa agreed.

It took forever to make their way back alongside the road. They were glad to see the houses of Santa Rosita Estates ahead, though it seemed to Lily Vanessa that something was different.

It wasn't until they returned to Aunt Van's with the empty cat cage that Lily Vanessa realized something was very wrong. "My brass bracelet is gone! The bracelet Ma Darice brought me from Africa!"

"Oh no!" Tricia said.

"Are you sure?" Becky asked.

"Yes," Lily Vanessa answered. She showed them her bare arm. "Only scratches from the bush. The bracelet's really gone. I must have caught it on that bush when I scratched myself."

"Guess we'll just have to go back there to find it," Becky said. "There's no other way."

Lily Vanessa tried to swallow the lump in her throat. "I guess so. I'm sorry, guys. I'm really sorry."

CHAPTER

5

Lily Vanessa stood at her aunt's kitchen sink with Becky and Tricia, gulping down glass after glass of water. Finally their thirst was quenched.

"I feel better," Lily Vanessa said. "But no way can we walk to Cat Woman's place again to find my bracelet."

"You're right about that," Tricia agreed. She set her water glass in the sink and lifted her long reddish blond hair off her neck. "Would you believe my hair's still damp!"

Becky lifted her long brown hair, too. "So is mine."

"I believe it," Lily Vanessa answered, glad her corn-row braids kept her hair off her neck. "I feel damp all over."

The answering machine had a message, and she turned it on. Maybe her aunt or uncle had left one for her.

A man's voice said, "This message is for Lily Vanessa Shields. This is Ted Iddings. I'm the youth pastor at Santa Rosita Community Church. I enjoyed your tape so much that I hope you'll sing a solo for our youth service this Sunday. In fact, we'd be honored. Please give me a call late this afternoon, if possible."

Having said that, he left the phone number.

"Hey, that was Bear!" Tricia yelled. "You're on!"

Lily Vanessa tried not to grin. "Guess so. I'll call him when you guys leave for your TCC meeting this afternoon."

"I can't wait to hear you sing," Becky said.

"Let's just hope I don't mess up," Lily Vanessa told them.

"You won't," Tricia promised. "We'll pray for you while you sing . . . if you want us to."

Lily Vanessa drew a breath of relief. "I sure do."

Quite suddenly, an idea hit. "Hey, Aunt Van and Uncle Raymond have bicycles in the garage, and I can use them. If we borrowed one of yours, we could ride to Cat Woman's."

"Sounds good, but we should ask our parents even if we forgot to before," Becky said. "And we'd have to be home in time for the four-thirty TCC meeting."

"You're right, we should have asked them from the beginning," Tricia said. "We just didn't think this would get so complicated. Let's phone now. We'll explain we have to find Lily Vanessa's bracelet. I have a feeling we better go *today*."

Despite her fear, Lily Vanessa did, too. "Aunt Van's in meetings. Maybe I can reach Uncle Raymond through his beeper."

They took turns on the phone and, surprisingly, both Tricia and Becky got permission to go.

When Uncle Raymond called back and Lily Vanessa told

him, he asked, "You mean that place with the huge goat?"

"It's where we took Cat. We'd be quiet—"

"Well, since it's that bracelet from Africa, I guess you should go. Just be careful."

"Believe me, we will," she answered.

He laughed. "And don't let that flea bag cat follow you back home, either."

She laughed herself. "We'll be careful of that, too."

They stopped at Tricia's house for her bike, then the three of them rode off down La Crescenta.

"Another adventure!" Tricia called out.

"Let's hope it's not another wild one," Lily Vanessa said.

"This time we'll be able to get away if that goat's around," Becky said. "We can ride faster than we can run."

Lily Vanessa hoped so.

Occasionally they had to pull off the road. But even with a car or two coming around the curves on High Road, it was easier to ride to Cat Woman's place than to stumble over gopher holes and through the brambles.

In fact, it was surprising to see how quickly they arrived at Cat Woman's driveway. They noticed that everything was overgrown on this end of the place, too. Even the "NO TRESPASSING" signs were tangled with bushes and vines.

Lily Vanessa braked her bike, waiting for the others to catch up. Nearby stood a crumpled mailbox nearly hidden with greenery. Even the mailbox door was barely clear of vines.

"Catch that mailbox," she told Becky and Tricia as they rode up on their bikes. "Looks as if a car or two has hit it."

"It sure does," Tricia agreed. "What's the name written under the vines?"

Lily Vanessa pushed the greenery aside. "Hmmm, Cat Woman's name is actually Ida Mae Burston."

Tricia raised her brows. "I don't think I've ever heard of Burstons, and I've lived over in Santa Rosita Estates all of my life. This property does sit alone way out here, though."

"I've heard the name Burston," Becky said.

"Ida Mae sounds old-fashioned and maybe southern," Lily Vanessa decided. "Probably she's old. Come on, maybe we'll see if Cat is happy. Let's hope she hasn't run away."

They pedaled their bikes up the driveway for some distance before being stopped by a solid white gate.

"No bell to ring or intercom system to call the house," Becky observed. "There're wheels under the gate, though."

Tricia hopped off her bike. "Maybe there's a latch on the other side."

She hurried to it and reached over. "Here it is. Just like the latch on our breezeway gate, but bigger." She rolled the gate open far enough for them to ride through, then closed it behind them.

Lily Vanessa looked around. "You know why this gate is way up on the driveway? It meets the wire fence, that's why. There's double fencing all around this place. And, look, all the shrubbery is neatly trimmed inside here, too. I'll bet the goat chews everything down."

"Let's get going before I chicken out," Becky advised.

Even the sounds of occasional cars on High Road disappeared as they biked farther into the property. The shaded driveway felt cool, but here and there sunshine glinted through the trees.

After a while, a dirt road veered left.

"This way," Lily Vanessa said. "This old road is like the

one we were on. It must go partway around the whole place."

As they rode on, they passed the rusty hulk of the red truck they'd seen on their first visit to the place. After a while, the trimmed trees and bushes along the road seemed familiar.

Lily Vanessa slowed her bike and eyed the taller bushes; green on top but the rest dried, maybe dead. With so many plants for the goat to eat, maybe he didn't bother with dead branches. She tried to remember where her bracelet had been snagged. It'd happened so fast—

"There!" Becky exclaimed. "There's your bracelet hanging on that bush! Can you believe it? The sun's shining right on it."

Not only that, the sun lit up hundreds of dusty cobwebs, Lily Vanessa noticed.

Deeper in the property, the dogs began to bark.

"Hurry!" Becky warned.

Lily Vanessa braked her bike to a wobbling stop, hopped off, and grabbed the bracelet, snagging only one cobweb. She wiped the web from her hand, jammed the bracelet into her pocket, and climbed back onto her bike.

"Here comes the goat!" Becky yelled.

Lily Vanessa glanced back. "Yikes!"

The goat barreled down the road at them.

Lily Vanessa pedaled wildly ahead of the others. Suddenly her front tire hit a deep rut and threw her head-over-heels through the air. She screamed as she flew into the dry underbrush for a scratchy landing. Her bike tumbled down the dusty road, falling sideways. Becky and Tricia couldn't stop fast enough to avoid her bike.

"Jump!" Lily Vanessa yelled at them.

They scrambled from their bikes and nearly knocked her down.

"Here comes the goat!" she shouted. Her eyes darted ahead to a weather-beaten shed. "Run for the shed!"

They ran wildly, finally reaching the shed.

"Hurry!" Lily Vanessa called out. She clambered up on a pile of old lumber, then helped Becky and Tricia up onto the shed's roof.

Horns lowered, the goat hit the dilapidated shed, butting it so hard the wood splintered.

"This shed's going to fall!" Becky cried out.

The goat backed up slowly, then lowered his head as if he meant to butt them to the moon.

"Get ready to jump!" Lily Vanessa cried. "Here he comes again!"

Suddenly three big dogs raced at him, barking hoarsely. Irritated, the goat stopped and turned toward the dogs.

Lily Vanessa, Becky, and Tricia clung to the shed roof, only slightly higher than the goat's head.

Ignoring the dogs, the goat turned his attention back toward the girls on the shed. He backed up and gathered his strength, then ran furiously at them again.

Lily Vanessa screamed.

The goat hit the shed hard, cracking boards under them.

"We've got to yell for help," Tricia said.

Lily Vanessa let loose with a loud "Help!"

"HELP!" they shouted above the dogs' furious barking. These were definitely mean watch dogs. "H-E-L-P! H-E-L-P!"

The goat backed up for another assault.

"H-E-L-P!" they shouted again.

In a flurry of white, a rope flew out from behind a tree, whizzing past them. A lasso! It settled with ease over the goat's neck.

A woman's voice croaked, "I got the noose on you again, you sorry old goat."

Huh? Lily Vanessa thought, even more shaken.

The voice shouted, "Don't tell me you ate through that other rope. You're a sly fella, ain't you, Brutus?"

A wiry, gray-haired woman emerged from behind the bushes. An old straw cowboy hat topped her tanned and wrinkled face, and she wore a tattered blue jeans outfit and old brown cowboy boots.

Whipping the rope expertly around a tree trunk, she announced, "Got you again, Brutus, didn't I?"

The goat stared at her as if he knew he was tied up now.

The woman patted the goat's head, calming him down.

She turned her pale blue eyes toward Lily Vanessa, Tricia, and Becky up on the shed. "You girls are trespassin' on my property. Didn't you see them 'no trespassing' signs?"

"We didn't mean any harm," Lily Vanessa replied. "We brought your cat back earlier today. At least we think it's your cat. My bracelet snagged on a bush, so I had to come back for it—"

"Lemme see that bracelet," the woman interrupted.

Lily Vanessa knelt on the roof of the shed and held her hand out to show the brass bracelet.

The woman raised her sharp chin. "It's a plain bracelet for all that trouble, ain't it?"

Lily Vanessa nodded. "It's plain, all right. But my grandmother brought it for me from Africa, so I didn't want to lose it."

The woman eyed her sternly now. Behind her, cats padded out from all around. Seeing them softened her expression. *Maybe she's one of those people who likes animals better than she likes people*, Lily Vanessa thought.

When no one spoke, she asked, "Are you Ms. Burston?"

"*Miss* Burston," the woman answered. "Miss Ida Burston. I don't hold with that *Ms.* talk."

Lily Vanessa tried again. "I hope you'll forgive us, but we figured Cat lived here, and then we had to come back for the bracelet—"

The woman gave her a hint of a smile. "Come to think of it, that white cat with orange and black splotches is back. And she came back mad."

"She's mad, all right," Lily Vanessa agreed.

"Had a thorn stuck deep in her left hind paw. Pulled it out for her, and she ain't so mad now."

Lily Vanessa gasped. "No wonder she was grouchy."

Becky and Tricia still sat on top of the shed, so she added, "I'm Lily Vanessa, and this is Becky and Tricia. They were trying to help me find the bracelet before the goat ran us up here."

"How do you do?" the woman replied, still eyeing them closely. "I reckon you kin call me Miss Ida. Why don't you come down off that shed now?"

"Thank you, Miss Ida," Lily Vanessa replied.

Becky asked, "You're sure Brutus won't butt us?"

"Or the dogs bite us?" Tricia added.

"Over my dead body," Miss Ida answered. "Them dogs and that billy goat obey me. Why, I raised every one of 'em—including that goat—right in my house." She ordered the dogs to the house, and after a few protest barks, they obeyed.

Turning back to the girls, her eyes went to Tricia and Becky. "Ain't I seen you two before? Maybe in the newspaper? Hey, you ain't some of the girls in that workin' club, are you?"

"We sure are," Tricia answered. "The Twelve Candles Club. Becky here is the president."

"Well, if that don't beat all!" Miss Ida exclaimed. "I was thinkin' of callin' you. My brother died up in L.A., and I have to go to his funeral tomorrow, but someone's got to see to all these animals. I read in the paper that you see to animals."

"We've done some dog-sitting," Tricia answered, "but . . . well, we've never taken care of so many animals at one time."

"It don't take much work," Miss Ida answered. "Mostly feedin' and givin' 'em water. There's only three dogs . . . and . . . well, lots of cats, and my goat, Brutus."

"Brutus?" Tricia asked.

Miss Ida nodded. "You know, like Brutus in the Popeye cartoons."

She rushed on. "It ain't hard work, and you could do it any time of the day you wanted. Not after dark, though, or you'll break your neck fallin' over roots or gopher holes. You could fit this job in between your other work."

"We're so busy these last two weeks before school starts," Becky explained. "Everyone wants us right now."

Tricia turned to Lily Vanessa. "At least two of us would have to be here together. Could you help us with the job?"

Lily Vanessa swallowed. "Me?"

Miss Ida's pale blue eyes lit up. "I'd make it worth you girls' while . . . I'd even pay double. It's my only brother who died. Since I'm taking one of them Amtrak trains to get there, I'd be back Saturday afternoon. Let's see, today is Thursday. It's only a day and a half."

Despite her reluctance, Lily Vanessa felt bad for the old woman. It wasn't just a matter of making money, but a feeling that she should help.

Miss Ida stuck a finger into a dusty cobweb and twirled the web around and around on her finger. "That's for good luck . . . so you'd take the job."

"What do you mean?" Lily Vanessa asked.

Miss Ida's eyes widened. "Why, don't you know? Twirling cobwebs brings luck."

Lily Vanessa thought they all must have looked at Miss Ida strangely because she gave a sudden laugh. "Ain't so lucky, though, if the cobweb has a black widow spider in it."

"Black widows are poisonous!" Lily Vanessa exclaimed. "Are there black widow spiders around here?"

"Yep," Miss Ida answered.

Lily Vanessa shivered. And Mom thought they had trouble with ants getting into their condo kitchen! She was about to say, "It's too dangerous for me," but Miss Ida kept talking.

"I ain't gonna lie to you about black widows being around . . . or anythin' else, either. I've never been a liar and don't plan on takin' it up now. There's black widows, scorpions, tarantulas, and rattlesnakes here and there. Keeps a person wide awake . . . on her toes, don't you know?"

Lily Vanessa shuddered.

Tricia asked, "Do you really twirl cobwebs for luck?"

"Yep," Miss Ida answered.

Ma Darice said Christians didn't believe in luck, Lily Vanessa thought. They believed in Jesus taking care of them.

She was grateful that Tricia said, "My gramp is a Christian minister, and he says anything about luck is superstitious. . . ."

The woman scowled. "I was raised a Christian, but them people didn't like me because I was different. I didn't want no more of it, so I just stopped goin' to church. Expect I'll have to listen in on my brother's funeral, but I won't like it."

"I'm sorry," Becky said. "Where did you go to church?"

"That church ain't around anymore. Closed up entirely."

"Are you a believer?" Tricia asked boldly.

Miss Ida raised her shoulders, then let them drop.

"I wish you'd come to Santa Rosita Community Church," Tricia told her. "We have lots of friendly people. You might even know some of them since you've always lived here. And you know what? Lily Vanessa is going to sing a solo Sunday."

Miss Ida's pale blue eyes flickered with interest, then she stared down at her boots. "I used to sing some."

"Like what?" Lily Vanessa asked.

"Church music, other kinds," Miss Ida answered. "Sang solos myself. Sang in the choir, too. My parents were church-goin' people."

She sounded regretful, Lily Vanessa thought. Maybe she should invite her to come Sunday, too, but it wasn't even her church.

As they talked, it turned out that Miss Ida had sung country western music, too, even with a band on weekends.

"I wish I could hear you sing," Lily Vanessa said.

"Them days are over," she answered. "Don't sing no more."

Becky said, "I'm afraid I can't help with the animals. My family's just moved across town, and I have to unpack the rest of my stuff."

Lily Vanessa knew what God wanted her to do. She made herself say, "I could come here and help with the animals. I'd do it if one of you came with me every time."

"I could help sometimes," Tricia offered, "but not if that goat chases us or the dogs take after us."

"I'll chain the dogs and Brutus, too," Miss Ida said. "Usually you can't chain goats or they'll choke, but Brutus is so big, it works just fine on him."

She added, "Like I said before, goats are right sociable animals if you keep more than one. Should've had another goat to keep Brutus company. Bein' alone made him downright mean."

Lily Vanessa wondered if Miss Ida might be different, too, if she weren't such a loner.

"Maybe we can do the job for you," Tricia said.

Miss Ida beamed. "Good! You're hired! I'll show you around now. You'll need to see where the animals' food and dishes are kept. You'll like Brutus when you get to know him. He's smart like most goats."

Lily Vanessa watched for rattlesnakes and other varmints as they followed behind Miss Ida along the twisting driveway. Up ahead in the garage stood an old tan pickup with a crumpled back fender. Must be Miss Ida's transportation.

"I'll feed 'em all before I leave," Miss Ida said. "You can start tomorrow morning. These animals are used to getting fed and watered three times a day—"

"Three times a day?!" Lily Vanessa echoed.

Miss Ida nodded. "Guess I spoil 'em."

"Yikes, I can't come tomorrow morning!" Tricia said. "We do a playcare—Morning Fun for Kids—on Fridays, and I always do an imaginary magic carpet ride with the Funners—"

"No way am I coming alone!" Lily Vanessa interrupted. "I'm not used to being way out in the country like this!"

"Maybe I could help then," Becky said. "That'd leave four TCCers for Morning Fun for Kids."

"I'd come at noon," Tricia promised Lily Vanessa. "And maybe Jess could help before her slumber party. We'll just need someone to come with you Saturday morning."

"Okay, I guess," Lily Vanessa said, feeling a little left out at the mention of Jess's slumber party.

In the garage, Miss Ida showed them where she kept cat and dog food, and oats for Brutus. "Carrots are in this old refrigerator, and I keep a spare key in this vegetable bin in case you have to get in the house for an emergency."

She added, "You'll have to move Brutus's chain to the next tree so he has new grass to graze on."

"We'd have to move him?" Lily Vanessa asked anxiously.

"It's easy with two of you," Miss Ida assured her. "One gives him carrots and oats, and while he's eating, the other one moves the chain to the next tree. I'll show you."

How did I ever get into this? Lily Vanessa asked herself. It was the craziest thing she'd ever agreed to do. But maybe she was meant to do it. Ma Darice would do it to help. So would Uncle Isaiah. She had an uneasy feeling, though, that there could be more to the job than just taking care of Miss Ida's animals. What was it?

CHAPTER

6

*L*ily Vanessa pedaled the bike along, glancing at the neighborhood's neat stucco, red-tile-roofed houses. Becky pedaled along on one side of her; Tricia rode on the other. It was decided that now they'd be "seeing to" Miss Ida's place until she returned.

"What are you singing at church Sunday?" Tricia asked.

Lily Vanessa shrugged, then looked down at her long feet pushing the bike pedals around and around. "I'm still waiting."

"What do you mean?" Becky asked.

Lily Vanessa gave her a little smile. "You're not going to believe this, but sometimes when my brain's freewheeling, I have sort of a radio playing in my head. You know, I wake up with a song, or it comes along later. I'm waiting now for God to put the right one in there for Sunday."

"Awesome!" Tricia exclaimed.

"What's playing in your head now?" Becky inquired.

Lily Vanessa almost laughed. "Nothing while I'm talking to you guys."

Tricia said a comical "I guess not!"—making them laugh.

After a while, Lily Vanessa grew serious. "Actually, 'Go Tell It on the Mountain' has been playing a lot lately. You know the one. . . ." She decided to sing out the words,

> "Go tell it on the mountain,
> over the hills and everywhere.
> Go tell it on the mountain
> that Jesus Christ is Lord!"

They were quiet, then Becky said, "That's what the youth group is singing at the end of the service."

"Oh," Lily Vanessa answered. "Then that isn't it."

"You have a great voice, though," Tricia put in kindly.

"Thanks." She remembered to add, "God gave it to me."

Tricia puffed out her cheeks, then gave her a closed-lipped smile as she rode alongside. "I'm glad I'm not the only one with interesting stuff going on in my head."

"What's been playing in yours?" Lily Vanessa asked.

"Usually stories and acting," Tricia replied.

"Like what?"

Tricia laughed. "You know, Character A yells, 'No way will I ever rob that bank!' and Character B answers, 'Listen, man, we've done a background check on you, and we say you'll do the bank hold-up!' "

Laughing, Becky said to Tricia, "You've never told me about that, Trish."

"I've never told anyone till now," Tricia returned. "It's not the kind of thing you usually tell others."

"Sounds like you have acting roles in your head," Lily Vanessa remarked, pedaling onward. "Maybe a TV show."

Tricia shook her head. "Usually it's stage acting. That was only a fast example."

"Since we're telling secrets," Becky began, "I'll tell you what goes on in my head."

No one spoke, so Becky continued. "Lots of times I see real things as if they're in pictures, and I decide how to paint them. A while ago we passed a white, gated wall covered with red flowers, and I thought, for a watercolor painting, the gate should be the main focus."

"Beck!" Tricia exclaimed. "Why haven't you told us before?"

"I think maybe I have," Becky objected, "but in a different way. I'd say, 'You know, that would make a good picture. Just look at the colors.' That kind of stuff."

Lily Vanessa smiled as she pedaled onward. "You guys are as crazy as I am. Wonder what it'd be like if everyone told what was going on in their heads."

"It'd be interesting from some people," Becky said, "but maybe not so good in others. I bet there are some that are totally empty."

They laughed at the idea.

After a while Tricia added, "Seriously, my gramp always warns to be sure it's God's voice you listen to, and not the enemy's. Gramp says the difference is that God always speaks in a still, small voice, and even then you should have godly people confirm it."

They pedaled on in silence.

Lord, what should I sing? Lily Vanessa asked silently.

Slowly, a song came to mind, right down to the arrangement. It was a still, small voice, but she'd get others to confirm it.

When they arrived at Aunt Van's house, Lily Vanessa parked the bike fast, let Tricia and Becky in the front door, and headed for the phone. The music in her brain wasn't changing.

Lord, if this is right, please let Becky and Tricia and their youth pastor confirm it.

She only said to them, "I'd better call your youth pastor . . . I mean Bear now. I . . . ah . . . think it'd be best for me to sing something everybody already knows."

"Like what?" Becky asked.

"Like 'Amazing Grace,' but I'd sing it black gospel style. You know, waking it up a little."

"Is that what's playing in your head now?" Tricia asked.

"It was just a few seconds ago," Lily Vanessa assured her. "Does your church sing it a lot?"

Tricia shook her head. "We sing mostly praise songs, not the old hymns too often. 'Amazing Grace' gospel style sounds perfect to me. Someone sang it like that once in Gramp's church, and it was so wonderful, I still remember."

Minutes later, Bear was on the phone. "Hey, Lily Vanessa, I like your name and your singing," he said. "I'm glad you can be with us Sunday morning."

"Thanks."

"What will you be singing?" he asked.

" 'Amazing Grace.' But I want to liven it up a little."

"Sounds great. Actually, you can liven it up a lot," he said. "What are you going to need for accompaniment?"

"I've got an accompaniment track, and it just so happens I brought it with me."

His voice held a big smile. "Sounds like God's been leading you right in this direction."

She felt a little strange, but she answered, "I really tried to listen to Him about choosing the song."

———

For dinner that evening, she just made a big tomato and lettuce salad, since there was plenty of leftover jambalaya for Aunt Van, Uncle Raymond, and her. She hadn't seen much of them for the past two days, and she looked forward to telling them all the news. She had the house smelling like jambalaya when they came home.

"Oh, does that smell good," her uncle declared. He inhaled deeply, a toothy smile lifting his cheeks. "I'd say it smells like it must smell in heaven. Come on, Van, let's hurry to the table before the world beats a path to our door to eat it all up."

At the table, after he'd said grace, he tried the jambalaya. His eyes widened and he slowly removed the fork from his mouth. "Ummm, that's mighty good cooking, girl. Where'd you learn to cook like that?"

"From Ma Darice," Lily Vanessa answered. "She's been teaching me to cook every chance she gets, ever since I was little. She'd say, 'A little more onion, a little more spice, a little more ham. . . . ' She's always a-little-more-of-this-or-that-ing at me."

"I can believe it," Aunt Van laughed. "But it's very good cooking. Lily, girl, you're going to make us fatter."

Lily Vanessa laughed. "You're not fat."

"Plump," her aunt said, laughing herself. "We're both round-faced and pleasingly plump. Why else would I be wearing this balloony blue dress?"

"You two look just right. Just like my aunt and uncle should," Lily Vanessa insisted.

Smiling, Aunt Van smoothed a hand over her neat French twist. "You did say the right thing there!" she exclaimed. "And I do believe you mean it."

"I do," Lily Vanessa answered.

Maybe her aunt and uncle were a trifle plump, but if all of her relatives were like them in most ways, the world would be a better place.

Her uncle said, "If I'd known you could cook like this, I'd have asked you to cook all last week."

"Me too," Aunt Van agreed.

They ate quietly for a while, then Uncle Raymond said, "I see you found your bracelet. Things all right at the Burston place? Everything go okay?"

"Fine," Lily Vanessa answered. "We even got a job there taking care of Miss Ida's animals while she's in L.A. for her brother's funeral."

"What animals?" Uncle Raymond asked.

She tried to look confident. "Cat and a hundred or so other cats, some dogs, and a goat."

"A goat?" Aunt Van echoed.

Lily Vanessa decided not to say how big of a goat. She rushed on. "I think Miss Ida's lonely. Since I'm singing Sunday, should I invite her to church?"

"That's always a good idea," her aunt replied.

Uncle Raymond asked, "You're singin' this Sunday, too?"

"Over at Santa Rosita Community Church," she told him and explained about Bear and Youth Sunday. "I thought you'd be glad, but maybe I should have asked permission about that, too."

Uncle Raymond beamed. "You should have, but you won't be hearin' any complaints from me."

"Nor from me!" Aunt Van put in. "Delighted to hear it."

"Could you do my hair up in a French twist exactly like yours?" Lily Vanessa asked her.

"Of course," Aunt Van said. "I'd be honored."

Her aunt's brown eyes met hers, and the message coming between them was love.

"As for takin' care of the Burston place," Uncle Raymond said, "it sounds as if you've already agreed to do it."

"We have," Lily Vanessa answered. "I'd guess Miss Ida is on her way to L.A. right now."

"I'll have to tell your mother if she calls," Aunt Van said, her forehead wrinkled up again.

A good thing Mom isn't phoning, Lily Vanessa thought. *A really good thing, or she'd start to worry.*

The phone rang while they were cleaning up after dinner, and Aunt Van picked it up in the kitchen.

"Ma Darice!" she exclaimed happily. "We've been talking about you. In fact, we've just finished off your recipe for jambalaya made by our girl here." Her aunt winked at her.

Lily Vanessa smiled as she loaded the dishwasher. Before long Aunt Van said, "Lily Vanessa is singing in another church here Sunday. Yes, at the community church where her new friends go. For the annual youth service. She's going to liven up 'Amazing Grace.' "

Her aunt listened awhile. "You know you're always welcome." After a while she laughed and handed over the phone. "Ma Darice is aching to talk to you."

"Hi," Lily Vanessa said into the receiver. She decided to sit down on a stool by the counter since Ma Darice was known to hold long conversations.

"Hey!" Ma Darice answered in her low, rich voice. "I hear it's all set, your singing again. There're bound to be signs and wonders and glory happening in Santa Rosita with you singing everywhere, girl."

Lily Vanessa laughed. "You're teasing."

"Only a little. I'm half serious, too."

It didn't take long before her grandmother had all of the news from her, including the adventure with the goat. And about Miss Ida Burston.

"What's wrong with her?" Ma Darice asked.

"The other girls and I talked about it. They say Miss Ida's sort of a hermit . . . you know, a loner. We think she's lonely, and that maybe that's why she has all of those animals there."

"Could be." Her grandmother quieted, which probably meant she was praying about the matter. "Does she know the Lord?"

"We don't know. I've been wondering if I should invite her to church. . . ."

"Why not?" Ma Darice asked. "Tell me, why not?"

Lily Vanessa shrugged, mostly to herself. "I'm new here. I'm only visiting."

"Jesus was new in town in lots of the places He visited,"

her grandmother answered. "He was only visiting, too. What do you think He'd do?"

Lily Vanessa drew a breath. "He'd tell her that He was the way to God, that He loved her, that He could be her best friend so she doesn't have to be lonely."

"What else?" Ma Darice prompted.

"That He can lead her to friends at a church."

Ma Darice gave a laugh. "Sounds as if He's telling you exactly what to do."

"Do you really think so?"

Her grandmother remarked, "Maybe that's the reason He's put you in Santa Rosita right now. You ever think of that?"

"No, I guess I hadn't."

Her grandmother added, "One thing, maybe. I think you're there to make friends with those girls I met the other night. What else might it be?"

"To sing in the churches."

"What else?"

"I already mentioned inviting Miss Ida to church."

Her grandmother's smile came through the phone. "Maybe even to lead that Miss Ida to the Lord."

Lily Vanessa didn't answer. The idea of leading a grown-up to the Lord seemed to be going too far. Way too far.

She was relieved when her grandmother started on a new subject. "Have you written your mom at her conference?"

"I meant to, but you know me and writing letters. Besides, she hasn't called."

"I expect she's trying to save money," her grandmother said. "She told me you need new school clothes."

Lily Vanessa admitted, "She did send me three post-cards from Denver."

"See, didn't I tell you she's trying to save money?" Ma Darice asked. "I'm going to give you your mom's hotel fax number. Take it down, write to her now, and you can have a letter to her first thing in the morning. Your uncle has a fax machine right in his office. I just talked to your mother and, girl, she's missing you."

"I've never written a fax letter," Lily Vanessa objected.

"It's just like any other kind," her grandmother answered. "Do it. By the way, I'll be driving down Saturday night so I can hear you sing Sunday morning."

"I'm glad, except you're such a good singer—"

"None of that now. Won't be my job to criticize. You know I'll be praying you through."

Lily Vanessa knew it was true. And that's what Tricia had promised, too.

"I'll be driving you home Sunday afternoon, and we'll pick up your mom at the airport. I have her flight number."

As usual, her grandmother was taking charge of things, but Lily Vanessa decided she didn't mind. "Great! See you then."

"I love you, girl," Ma Darice said.

"Love you, too."

"Ooooh, that's nice to hear. See you Saturday night."

———

In her room, Lily Vanessa plopped onto the bed to start Mom's letter. Uncle Raymond had agreed to fax it to Denver first thing in the morning. There was only the writing to do.

Dear Mom,
   I know we'll both be home Sunday night, but thought I'd write to let you know the news. . . .

She read through the letter and decided it was all right. No sense going into details about Miss Ida Burston or anything else to worry Mom. It was hard enough for her to have Dad in the navy stationed way over in Italy.

A new thought struck.

Why was it that when she and Mom were together they had mom-and-kid troubles? But when they were apart, she missed her so much! It didn't make sense.

Something else didn't make sense. Everything seemed to be going along so well that a strange feeling was beginning to build in her. It was like Mom always warned. Maybe this was "the calm before the storm." Maybe "the excitement" was just ahead of her.

CHAPTER

7

The next morning, Lily Vanessa sat at the kitchen counter eating corn flakes with skim milk and strawberries. Aunt Van sat beside her spooning up the last of her shredded wheat.

Uncle Raymond had already eaten breakfast, and now he came in the front door carrying the morning newspaper. "Feels like those hot Santa Ana winds again," he said. "Devil winds, the Indians used to call them, they make people act weird."

Finished with breakfast, Aunt Van got down from her counter stool. "They sure do seem to affect my students every fall. Let's hope we're done with those winds before school starts."

Lily Vanessa knew about the winds herself. Every year they whipped across the deserts, bringing their hot air to L.A., too. And they did seem to make people crazier.

"Let's hope there aren't any wildfires here," Uncle Raymond said. "The grasses and trees are so dry."

The Santa Ana winds brought fires, Lily Vanessa knew. Last fall, huge fires had burned in Cleveland National Forest, and the smoke had blown all the way to the city. Raging fires had been shown on the TV news for a week.

Before long, her aunt and uncle hurried off to work. Aunt Van called behind her, "Be sure to check your church dress to see if it needs washing or ironing."

"I will!" Lily Vanessa replied. It was already Friday, so she'd have to get right on it.

She put the dishes in the dishwasher, then headed for her room. Her Sunday dress hung in the closet: a white cotton with graceful blue swirls, cap sleeves, a V-neck, and a gathered skirt. It was just right for church, not a spot on it, and last Sunday's wrinkles had already hung out. Perfect.

At nine o'clock she rode out of the garage on Aunt Van's red bike. Whew, the wind was hot for so early in the morning.

She glanced down the street.

No sign of Becky. No traffic, either. It was a quieter neighborhood than hers in L.A. A movement in the sky made her glance up, and she saw a red-tailed hawk circling a tall eucalyptus tree. Sure didn't see hawks at home.

As she closed the garage door, the phone rang in the house. By the time she'd unlocked the front door and ran to the kitchen phone, no one answered. Only a dial tone.

She hurried back outside, locking up behind her.

Still no Becky. What if she couldn't come after all? That meant feeding the animals alone. The Burston place was so wild, she'd be scared to go—but there was no way out of it now. A good thing she'd worn jeans to keep her legs away from black widow spiders, scorpions, and the rest of the scary stuff.

"Hey, Lily Vanessa!" Becky yelled, riding Tricia's bike down the street. She'd worn jeans, too.

Lily Vanessa waved at her in relief. "All right!"

When Becky rode up, she added, "Tricia's mom tried to call you to say I'd be late. I brought crafts and art supplies to Morning Fun for Kids, and it took a few minutes to explain how to use them. Sorry."

"I thought maybe it was you calling when I heard the phone. Am I glad you came!"

Becky smiled as she braked the bike to a stop. "Notice, I wore my cowboy boots in case of *varmints*."

"Don't even mention them!" Lily Vanessa climbed on the red bike. "I only have these tennies and my white patent leather shoes for Sunday here. Besides, I don't own cowboy boots. I used to have some, about four shoe sizes ago."

"I know the feeling," Becky said. "I'm glad I'm not the only one with big feet here."

Lily Vanessa laughed. "*Long feet* sounds more hopeful. You know, that maybe we'll grow up tall and thin like models, although Mom says our family doesn't have 'lasting thin genes.' We start out skinny, though."

Becky laughed with her. "I guess we don't have lasting thin genes either."

Still smiling, Lily Vanessa pedaled down the driveway. "Let's go, long feet!"

They rode off together down the street. Once in a

while gusts of wind blew grit at them, then the wind quieted.

"It's hot already," Becky said.

"At least the air's dry, not sticky."

They rode through the southern corner of Santa Rosita Estates, then took the lightly traveled cutoff to Hill Road.

Becky asked, "You want me to lead?"

"Good idea." Lily Vanessa slowed until Becky rode ahead. "I still don't know my way around here that well."

Occasionally cars came around the curves on Hill Road, but it was a pleasant bike ride. Here and there, houses stood down among lemon groves, and nearly all of the driveways were lined with colorful geraniums, bougainvillaea, or other flowers. A few empty lots held only golden brown grasses that waved in the wind.

"There's Cat Woman's driveway," Lily Vanessa called up to Becky. "Oops! I mean Miss Ida's."

"I'm trying to remember to call her Miss Ida, too," Becky admitted. "It's hard when everyone around here has called her Cat Woman for ages."

The driveway entrance looked the same as yesterday: overgrown bushes and trees, and the "NO TRESPASSING" signs and mailbox tangled with vines.

Lily Vanessa hopped off her bike to unlatch the big white driveway gate and pushed it open. She looked around. No sign of Brutus. "Let's hope the dogs and old Brutus are still on their chains. I don't want to be bitten or butted this morning."

They rode through the gate, then rolled it shut and pedaled down the driveway.

"I still can't believe I agreed to do this," Lily Vanessa said.

"We felt sorry for her, remember?"

Lily Vanessa nodded. "And I can use the money."

Before long, the sounds of cars on High Road disappeared, and it was cooler riding under the trees. "At least things are beginning to look familiar."

"Down that road is where the bush snagged my bracelet."

"And where Brutus charged us yesterday," Becky added.

Lily Vanessa laughed. "I've never in my life run that fast. Maybe I should take up sprinting in school."

Becky laughed. "Cara wishes she had a video of it. She sold a video tape to one of the TV stations this summer."

"It would have been funny, all right. She could probably get it on one of those wild home video shows."

Before long, their bikes bounced over more hardened ruts. "Yikes! The dogs are barking. I hate that sound."

The barking came from near the house, and now hordes of cats came out in a silent welcome. It was a spooky sight.

"Look, here comes Cat," Lily Vanessa said, slowing her bike in the dirt.

Becky braked her bike to a dusty stop. "She doesn't look mad, either."

"She's not," Lily Vanessa agreed, stopping her bike, too. She looked all around them. "Things might seem familiar, but it's still a little creepy here."

Becky nodded, then they rode on slowly together on the narrow driveway to the old garage and house.

Lily Vanessa had scarcely seen the house yesterday because the dogs had barked so fiercely around them while Miss Ida gave directions. Today she noticed that the house might once have been nice. The outside was now a dingy white and the paint was peeling. On top, the roof sagged.

By the time they parked their bikes, all three of the dogs barked out a harsh chorus. "Guess I'd complain, too, if I were chained to a tree," she decided.

"It doesn't seem fair that they're chained," Becky agreed. "Probably Miss Ida couldn't afford to take them to a kennel. Anyhow, she'll be back tomorrow night. I wish she'd had time to tell us their names.

"Quiet!" Becky yelled at the dogs. "We'll feed you soon."

"Be quiet, dogs!" Lily Vanessa added, calming them slightly. "Miss Ida says we should feed the cats first so they don't get into the dog food."

The garage looked even more dilapidated than the house, Lily Vanessa thought as she lifted the garage door. At least it slid overhead easily, but dust sifted down on top of their heads. She brushed it off her face, then bent over and shook her head to get the dust off.

Inside the garage, junk was piled everywhere. Nearby stood the bag of oats for Brutus and the old, scratched-up refrigerator. In the back, a wooden workbench held cans and bags of pet food—and lots of fresh spider webs.

"Let's work together," Becky suggested.

"Okay. Ummmm . . ." She spotted the big bags of pet food and saw one away from the spider webs. "There's the cat food. I'll get it. There shouldn't be any mice around here!"

"Not with all of those cats," Becky agreed. "I'll get the milk from the refrigerator."

Lily Vanessa shouldered a heavy bag of food and headed for the cats' food dishes lined up on the nearby stone path.

The dogs barked again.

"Quiet!" she yelled, but it didn't help. Probably they were wilder than ever because of the hot wind. Maybe they should have fed them first, no matter what Miss Ida said.

Now the cats crowded all around her as she filled each dish three-quarters full, just as Miss Ida had told them. "Get away, cats! Out of the way so I can pour this!"

Becky followed with a gallon of milk. "Here's your milk, cats. Stop that crowding or I'll spill it all over you!"

Finally the row of cat's dishes was filled with dry food and milk—and surrounded by hungry cats lapping it up.

"It's a wonder the coyotes don't eat the cats," Becky remarked. "Maybe the dogs keep them away."

"You mean there are coyotes here?" Lily Vanessa asked.

Becky nodded. "There usually are in canyons like these. There're owls up in the tall trees, too. They swoop down at night to catch mice, and they'll kill any cat who tries to beat them to the mice. They break cats' necks."

Lily Vanessa was suddenly glad the dogs were barking. At least they offered protection from coyotes. "We just have a fish tank at home. I don't know much about dogs or other pets, either."

"I know a little about dogs," Becky said. "I have an old

collie named Lass. What we better do is put the dogs' dry food and water in those dishes in the garage, then carry them over. Believe me, they'll stop barking when we feed them."

"Let's hope so!"

Once the dog dishes were filled, she and Becky carried the dishes and a bucket of water down the path to the excited dogs. They jumped and strained at their chains, finally quieting when Becky slid their dishes of food near them. They began to gobble their food greedily.

"Feeding so many animals must cost Miss Ida lots of money," Lily Vanessa remarked.

"You're right, it must," Becky answered. "Hey, we're almost done."

"Just Brutus yet," Lily Vanessa added as they made their way back to the garage for his oats. "We've saved the worst for last. Too bad he doesn't have another goat for company, like Miss Ida said. The way he acts, it's hard to believe that goats can actually be sociable."

Lily Vanessa got five carrots from the refrigerator, and Becky scooped his metal dish through the bag of oats. Ready, they carried the dish behind the house since Brutus was chained to a tree some distance away. There he was, grazing on the grass. He'd already munched on the tree's leaves as high as he could reach.

"Watch out for snakes!" Lily Vanessa warned.

"Don't mention it or the other varmints, either!"

They laughed uneasily, drawing the goat's attention.

"Yikes!" Becky said. "Brutus is lowering his head. What if he comes after us?"

"He's on a strong chain," Lily Vanessa replied.

His chain reached out from the big trunk of a California pepper tree. His horns gleamed and he stared at the girls. Suddenly he lowered his head and ran at them.

"Yikes, here he comes! Run!!!"

They ran wildly toward the driveway as Brutus charged. "WHOOFFF!"

They glanced back. "Whew!" Becky said. "The chain held him! Sounds like it half-choked him, too."

Lily Vanessa was glad she hadn't spilled the carrots and oats from his dish when she ran. "He's a little winded."

They waited to be sure he couldn't pull his chain farther toward them. No, it was as far as he could go.

"This is some kind of job," Lily Vanessa complained.

"I'll think a little harder before agreeing to anything like this again!" Becky added.

They stood watching Brutus, and he stared back as if daring them to come closer.

Lily Vanessa asked, "Who's going to give the dish of oats to him? And who's going to chain him to that next pepper tree? To tell the truth, I don't want to do either!"

Becky drew a breath. "I'll rechain him if you push the dish to him. You can do it with your foot. Maybe he'll shorten your foot for you!"

Lily Vanessa gave a laugh. "Come on!"

Becky laughed with her, then they grew serious.

"I'll put the dish down here and keep him busy while you move the chain."

"Okay," Becky agreed. "I'll go around to the first tree."

Lily Vanessa made herself smile at Brutus. "Here, Brutus . . . here's some fine oats for you." She held out the dish of carrots and oats, which he eyed with interest. "See, treats!"

"I'll go now," Becky said, then started for the next big pepper tree.

Brutus began to follow her, and Lily Vanessa held the dish of oats toward him, backing around. "Now?" she asked, enticing him back. "Should I give it to him now?"

"Keep tempting him with it till I get to the tree," Becky replied. "I'll let you know when to give it to him."

"Okay."

Brutus lowered his head to attack.

"Calm down," Lily Vanessa told him, hoping he wouldn't break his chain. "You'll have your goodies in a minute."

She called over to Becky, "He's getting mad. I don't know how much longer I can keep his attention."

Becky ran for the tree, undid the loop of chain, then yelled, "Now!"

Lily Vanessa set the bowl near him, then nudged the bowl closer to him with her foot. "Here's your treat, Brutus."

He gave an angry bleat, a deep-voiced "Maaaaaah!"

She pushed the bowl closer, hoping he wouldn't sink his teeth or his sharp horns into her tennie.

Finally, he bent over the bowl and began to eat.

"Nice Brutus," she told him loudly enough for Becky to hear. "Nice Brutus, eating his oats this morning."

Some distance behind him, Becky hurried with the chain to the next pepper tree. The chain clinked a little as she ran across the grass, but Brutus was eating too greedily to notice. At long last, she looped the chain around the second tree.

"It's done!" she called out. "The chain's on this tree." Lily Vanessa stepped back in relief, forgetting the clump of bushes behind her, and backed right into a web.

She screamed, brushing at the web wildly. "I'll bet there's a black widow spider on me!"

Becky raced across the grass, and Brutus, forgetting his oats, took off after her.

"Run!" Lily Vanessa yelled, shivering and wildly brushing off the spider web.

Becky swerved out of Brutus's reach at the last moment and nearly ran Lily Vanessa down.

After they'd caught their balance, Becky gasped, "Let's see that web. Hold still!"

Lily Vanessa shuddered and made herself stand still.

"It's just a dusty old cobweb," Becky said. She brushed the rest of it from Lily Vanessa's back and shoulders. "There hasn't been a spider in it for months, I'll bet."

"I don't care if there hasn't been a spider in it for twenty years," Lily Vanessa answered and shivered. "It feels disgusting."

"It's all off now," Becky assured her. "And we've got the morning feeding job done. Actually it was sort of fun."

"Fun?" Lily Vanessa repeated.

Becky grinned. "Didn't you think it was?"

"No way! I'm not a country girl like you."

Becky laughed. "Well, maybe I am the most country of us," she said, "but I'm not used to something *this* wild."

Lily Vanessa felt too relieved to discuss the subject further. "At least we've lived through our first time here."

Becky laughed. "We did, didn't we?"

Lily Vanessa managed a smile. She definitely did not want to think about the next pet feeding.

CHAPTER

8

When the phone rang, Lily Vanessa was belting out the first notes of "Amazing Grace." She caught the phone on its third ring. "Hello!"

On the other end, a familiar voice said, "Hi, it's me, Tricia. I have an emergency. I'm still going to help you at the Burston place, but I have to baby-sit Jojo and Jimjim Davis this afternoon, too. Mrs. Davis will drop us all off at Miss Burston's, and my mom will pick us up in an hour."

"You're bringing little kids with you?!" Lily Vanessa asked with amazement. "How old are they?"

"Five years old. But it's really an emergency. Mrs. Davis's uncle was just taken to the hospital, and she has to be there until his other relatives get into town."

Tricia hesitated. "We just feed the animals canned food and see that they have plenty of water, isn't that all?"

"That's it for this feeding. But it makes me nervous to

think about you bringing kids there."

"What could go wrong in an hour?" Tricia asked. "Anyhow, they're characters. They even talk in a secret twin language."

They do sound fun, Lily Vanessa thought. Maybe she was making too big of a deal of the kids being there. Actually, things had gone well this morning. "You're probably right."

"Great! See you," Tricia answered.

Minutes later, a car horn sounded from the driveway. Lily Vanessa ran out and saw Tricia in the front seat with a woman driver, and kids in the backseat. Tricia stuck her head out and yelled, "It's just us!"

"Hi," Lily Vanessa said as she climbed into the backseat. Tricia introduced her to Mrs. Davis, who looked friendly but frazzled. Maybe because her twin boys in the backseat looked so mischievous.

Tricia said, "Those cute boys back with you are Jojo and Jimjim. They're five years old. You want me to sit in the back with them? I didn't think about where we'd sit—"

"No problem," Lily Vanessa answered. She buckled up fast, since Mrs. Davis was already backing the car from the driveway.

Lily Vanessa glanced at the boys. They wore identical green and white outfits with their names stitched on them: *Jojo* and *Jimjim*. Identical twins for sure. Green eyes, dark curly hair, and freckles.

"Hi, guys," she said to them.

The boys' green eyes glinted at her with curiosity. They probably weren't around black people often. In fact, she'd no more than sat back when Jojo touched her arm and glanced at his finger.

She laughed. "The color doesn't rub off."

As they drove down the street, she put a finger on the tip of his nose, then looked at her finger. "Your freckles don't come off, either."

Jojo smiled and called past her to Jimjim, "Umpty-dumpty-um-dum-a-lum!"

The boys laughed wildly, and Lily Vanessa sat back again, grinning herself. It was twin language for sure. She said, "I bet you guys are lots of fun."

"They are," Tricia put in. "They're lots of fun to baby-sit, except you don't dare let them sit on a desk chair with wheels if they can find a dog to pull them down a driveway."

"So, you're the guys who did that?" Lily Vanessa asked them. "You rode a desk chair down a steep driveway?"

They nodded proudly.

After a moment Tricia and Mrs. Davis began to discuss final baby-sitting arrangements, so Lily Vanessa made funny faces with the twins.

After a while Tricia said, "Guys, tell her about how your room's decorated."

Jimjim said, "Elephants."

"Elephants?" Lily Vanessa repeated, and they nodded. "Real elephants like at the zoo? Or in Africa?"

"Different elephants," Jojo explained.

"Different elephants," Jimjim repeated.

"Sounds interesting," Lily Vanessa responded. "You know, in Africa they have real elephants. My grandmother was there and just brought home some tiny carvings of elephants . . . and this bracelet, too."

The boys examined her brass bracelet, and seeing the mischievous glint in their eyes, she held on to it.

"Their room looks a lot like Africa must," Mrs. Davis said. "One wall has a whole herd of elephants painted on it."

"Sounds wonderful," Lily Vanessa told the twins. "I'd take that room myself."

Minutes later, they pulled up at the Burston driveway. "I'll open the gate," Lily Vanessa said.

She jumped out, undid the latch, and rolled the white, wooden gate open on its rollers.

"We'll get out here," Tricia told Mrs. Davis. "It'd be hard to back your car out, and you're in a hurry." She quickly climbed out and opened the door for the boys.

Mrs. Davis remarked through her open window, "This is quite a neatly trimmed place inside the gate."

"Thanks to a goat named Brutus," Tricia answered.

"A goat!" Mrs. Davis repeated. "One doesn't think of having a goat around here nowadays."

The girls nodded, and, distracted, Mrs. Davis warned her twins, "Now, you boys behave. Be sure to stay away from the animals."

As she backed the car out, she added, "I really appreciate you girls baby-sitting Jojo and Jimjim this afternoon. I'll be home just as soon as possible."

They all waved, then the boys helped Tricia and Lily Vanessa roll the dingy white gate shut. Down below, the dogs were already barking.

"Dogs!" the boys yelled.

"Yep, it's dogs, all right," Lily Vanessa answered.

"They're watch dogs," Tricia told the boys as they all started down the driveway. "They're not friendly, so stay away from them. We don't touch these pets."

The next moment, the boys took off running.

Tricia and Lily Vanessa tore after them, each grabbing one of the twins.

"No more of that," Tricia warned them. "We go to the garage first."

As they neared the garage, cats emerged from all over. "Cats!" Jojo announced.

Jimjim said, "Want to pet the cats."

"If you boys are good and stand back," Tricia told them, "we'll let you feed the cats. There're three dogs here, too, and a big, old white goat."

Jimjim asked, "A real goat?"

"Yes, a billy goat," Tricia told them. "Remember that story about the billy goats who were gruff? He has a beard, too, like in the pictures of the Billy Goats Gruff."

The boys' faces lit up with excitement. Probably they'd seen goats on TV, too.

"I'll open the cat food cans so you can supervise the boys," Lily Vanessa suggested.

In the garage she counted out twenty-five cans of cat food and took them down from the shelf. She started opening one can after another, glad for the electric can opener, and Tricia and the boys carried the cans over to the line-up of cat dishes along the walk.

When the cats were finished, Lily Vanessa uncoiled the garden hose, sprayed out their dishes, and refilled them with water. Except for the dogs barking endlessly, things were going well, she decided.

Back in the garage, she opened the canned dog food.

"You boys stay away from the dogs," Tricia warned again. "Dogs can be mean when they're chained up. You can fill up that bucket of water for them. I'll turn on the hose for you."

Jojo and Jimjim's green eyes danced with mischief.

Lily Vanessa felt sure they'd spray them. Instead, they whispered to each other.

"Where's the goat?" Jojo asked.

"We feed him last," Lily Vanessa answered, deciding not to divulge Brutus's location.

"What's his name?" asked Jimjim.

"Brutus," Lily Vanessa told them. "Like Brutus in the Popeye cartoons."

Surprisingly, they behaved well while she and Tricia fed the dogs and refilled their water bowls.

"Now we're going to feed Brutus some oats and give him fresh water," Lily Vanessa told them.

They jumped up and down. "Want to see Brutus! Want to see Brutus!"

"Hold everything!" she told them. "Are the Santa Ana winds making you crazy, too?"

Returning to the garage, she got a handful of carrots from the old refrigerator, then filled a dish with oats. Tricia had already filled a bucket with water.

"This way behind the house," Lily Vanessa told them. "Becky and I already moved Brutus this morning."

Some distance behind the house they saw Brutus eating grass. He turned toward them, still munching.

"Yikes, he's knocked over his water dish," Lily Vanessa said. "Miss Ida stressed how important it was to give him water."

"We'll have to give him some," Tricia replied.

Lily Vanessa surveyed the scene. Brutus had stopped

munching and was heading toward them. "Miss Ida said if one of us keeps him here, feeding him treats, the other could refill the water."

"I'll refill the water dish," Tricia offered. "With all of my acting experience, I figure I can fool an old goat."

"Fine with me," Lily Vanessa replied with relief.

That decided, Tricia started off, carrying the bucket of sloshing water.

Lily Vanessa and the boys waved their arms and yelled, trying to keep Brutus's interest as he slowly approached.

The twins yelled, "Brutus is coming!"

"That's just what we want," Lily Vanessa told them.

The boys edged behind a nearby clump of wire-encircled bushes and an old pepper tree.

Probably scared, she decided. At least they'd be out of Brutus's reach.

"Here, Brutus!" she called to him. "Here's some nice oats and carrots for you! What a treat oats and carrots must be when you've just been eating grass and bushes."

Brutus chewed thoughtfully as he ambled along toward them. Suddenly Jojo and Jimjim scrambled up the big pepper tree. "Boys, what are you doing?" she demanded.

"Climbing the tree so Brutus can't get us!" one yelled.

"Shhhhh!" she warned. "I don't know if goats climb trees, and I don't want to find out now, either! We'll move him from here in a while."

Brutus eyed the boys, who straddled a low, sturdy branch in the pepper tree. Then the goat ambled toward her again.

She watched Brutus nearing her at the end of his chain. In the distance, Tricia was almost to his water dish.

Lily Vanessa threw two carrots to him. "Here, Brutus!"

His ears perked up, and he walked over, right under the pepper tree, and lowered his head—this time not to butt, but to munch on the carrots.

Suddenly Jojo and Jimjim shouted, "Ride 'em, cowboy!" They leapt off their branch and right onto Brutus's back just like bronco riders. One twin slipped off and tumbled away, but the other grabbed Brutus's ears and yelled, "Giddy-up, Brutus! Giddy-up!"

Lily Vanessa screamed as Brutus reared up and flung the second twin off his back and onto the grass.

She threw the other carrots and oats at the goat's head, getting his attention. Then she ran over to the two boys, who were frightened but not hurt.

"Boys, run toward the garage! Run!"

Tricia came yelling from across the yard, further distracting Brutus, while the boys scrambled up from off their backsides and raced away.

"You boys!" Lily Vanessa yelled, running after them.

They checked the boys over one more time, and noticed their mischievous looks had been replaced with something that looked more like relief.

Brutus looked up at them all, perplexed. It was as if he were thinking the same thing that she was: *What will happen next?*

———

At four o'clock, Jess rode her bike up Aunt Van and Uncle Raymond's driveway. "Ready to go feed Miss Ida's zoo?"

Lily Vanessa walked her bike from the garage. "Ready.

In fact, I'm ready for almost anything after what we've been through there."

Jess laughed. "Sounds like you and Tricia had lots of excitement with Jojo and Jimjim."

"You know it."

The bike ride to Miss Ida's was fun, and Lily Vanessa retold the noontime adventure with Jojo and Jimjim. "Let's hope this feeding is calmer," she said. "I can understand now why my mom says we're turning her hair gray. You see any gray in my hair?"

Jess laughed. "It's hard to see gray in corn-row braids. Why do you keep your hair that way?"

"It's cool in the summer," Lily Vanessa answered, pedaling alongside her. "Besides, my hair is really dry. I mean *almost no oil at all.*"

"Maybe you should stand on your head like I do," Jess said with a laugh. "Some gymnasts say it's a good way to get your hair oil to the top of your head."

Lily Vanessa chuckled. "I'll bet." She was beginning to feel more comfortable with Jess, and with the other TCCers, too. "I'm going to wash my hair when I get home. It smells awful from all the smoke in the air."

"Think I'll wash mine, too," Jess replied. "I hate these Santa Ana winds and fires."

When they arrived at the Burston place, everything seemed normal. The cats streamed out from the bushes, the dogs barked, and Brutus was grazing.

"It's a weird place," Jess remarked.

"I'm getting more used to it."

Before long, the cats and dogs were fed. Brutus must be getting accustomed to them, too, she decided, not even lowering his head to butt. Either that, or the weather was just too hot.

As they finished their job, Jess said, "That was okay."

"And better yet," Lily Vanessa said, "only one more feeding, tomorrow morning."

They locked the gate behind them and took off riding. Far away, they heard the siren of fire engines, and a column of smoke rose in the sky in the distance.

"Another fire," Jess said.

"We have Santa Ana winds in L.A. too, but there's not much countryside to burn around my neighborhood."

"There's still open land around here," Jess said. "Right here at Miss Ida's and along Hill Road. Just think of all of those oily eucalyptus trees bursting into flames."

"Don't even talk about it!" Lily Vanessa answered.

They rode along in the hot wind, mostly in silence.

As they pedaled into Santa Rosita Estates, Jess said, "Hey, how'd you like to come to my slumber party tonight? Mom's buying pizza, and we'll probably practice a little for tomorrow. You know, the church Youth Sunday program."

"Sure, I'd love to!" Lily Vanessa said with amazement. "I'll have to ask my aunt, though."

Jess beamed. "We don't have any black friends, and we'd like to get to know you better."

Lily Vanessa's spirits drooped low.

Was she an exhibit . . . just an exhibit?

But maybe God had chosen her to be one.

Ma Darice claimed that was how people of different races got to know each other. One by one, little by little.

Lord, Lily Vanessa prayed, *help me to show your love to my new friends, no matter the color of their skin. And help me to smile when people stare, no matter how much I dislike it.*

————

At six o'clock, she biked through the smokey air to the next street, La Crescenta, and then to Jess's house. Aunt Van and Uncle Raymond were pleased that she'd been invited, since some of the neighbors were just plain unfriendly to them.

"It's good for us to stretch our horizons," Aunt Van had said, sounding like a teacher, as usual.

Uncle Raymond said, "Here, take along this bag of chocolate kisses. Everyone will enjoy them. There's nothin' like food for makin' friends."

"And laughing," Lily Vanessa had replied.

Aunt Van had smiled. "And laughter," she agreed. "Scripture says, 'A merry heart doth good, like medicine.'"

Lily Vanessa glanced at her watch now, not wanting to arrive too early. Six o'clock on the dot seemed just right, and that's when Jess had told her to come. She checked her white tee and white denim shorts; it was a safe kind of outfit to wear to a slumber party. She'd washed her hair, and Aunt Van had replaited the corn-row braids.

Riding along, she hoped the chocolate kisses wouldn't melt. Ocean breezes usually blew cool air inland late in the afternoons, but there'd been no cool ocean winds lately. Worst of all, the smell of ashes was everywhere.

Arriving at Jess's house, she slowed her bike.

It was the biggest house in Santa Rosita Estates, maybe because Jess's dad was an airline pilot and her mother was a realtor. The red-roofed house covered two lots and stood higher from the street than any of its neighbors.

She glanced around for the other TCCers, but none were in sight, so she started to pedal up the driveway.

Moments later, Cara yelled from across the street. "Wait up, I'm on my way."

Lily Vanessa waited, glad for company.

Cara hurried up the driveway. "I'll show you where to park your bike behind the garage. Jess's puppy is back there, and he'll bark if anyone comes around. We had a burglar here in June."

"Scary!" Lily Vanessa commented.

Cara nodded. "It sure is. We're not used to burglars or other bad guys in this neighborhood."

They walked her bike around the garage, and she was glad to see the brown chow puppy. He was as cute as could be, except for his high-pitched yipping.

"Quiet, Tumbles!" Cara told him. "Quiet!"

Finally he quieted.

"It must be nice to live in a halfway safe neighborhood," Lily Vanessa remarked. "We don't live in the inner city, but crime is spreading where we live now. We can't leave bikes out anywhere, that's for sure."

"I . . . I hope you didn't misunderstand what I meant. . . ."

Smiling, Lily Vanessa parked her aunt's bike. "Cara Hernandez, I think you're way too sensitive to say anything hurtful on purpose."

Cara shook her head. "Thanks, but not always—especially not with my sister. I'm still learning 'a gentle word turns away wrath.' "

"You're not the only one learning that."

Understanding, they smiled at each other.

"Come on," Cara said, then led the way around the front of the new garage. "Jess has her own front door since her room was remodeled from what used to be a three-car garage. Wait till you see."

Just then a car pulled into the driveway and Becky climbed out. "Wait for me, guys!"

"Whew, smell that smoke," Cara remarked.

Lily Vanessa nodded.

As Becky approached, Cara said, "Look, you can actually see ashes in the air now."

Lily Vanessa didn't want to see or hear about it.

Jess met them at her door, her face glum. "Bad news, guys. There are fires all over in the hills. It's on the news right now. The winds are blowing trucks, trailers, and camper trucks over . . . uprooting big trees—"

"Turn that stuff off!" Becky said in her presidential voice. "Let's talk about something else. This is a slumber party, and we're going to have fun."

Lily Vanessa hoped so. She surely hoped so.

CHAPTER

9

Whoa!" Lily Vanessa exclaimed as she walked into Jess's room. It was really different.

In the far corner stood a twin bed corner unit, an old wooden coffee table, an old trunk, a chest of drawers, and a desk with a green chalkboard over it. The TV, blaring news about the fires, stood over near the closet and a clothes tree. The rest of it was what was so surprising: blue floor mats, a small trampoline, a gymnast's balance beam and vaulting horse, a ballet barre in front of a huge mirror, and on the high walls, huge posters of Olympic gymnasts.

Jess smiled. "I'm really serious about gymnastics."

"I guess so!"

"Come on, let's sit down on the floor cushions or the beds in the corner," Jess said, leading the way.

She added, "I have chips, dip, and veggies out on the

table. Notice my new—I mean *old*—coffee table and floor cushions. I found them at a junk store yesterday, and Mom still hasn't forgiven me for buying them. I think they look right with the really old trunk from my gold rush relatives."

"They give the room a homier feeling," Becky said. "Old things always do."

"Good," Jess said, "that's what I want." She dashed over to turn off the television.

"Becky's gram is an interior designer," Cara told Lily Vanessa. "She knows this kind of stuff. I'm never sure of what goes together, but I try."

"I don't know much about it, either," Lily Vanessa admitted. "Anyhow, my aunt says you wrote a winning essay in the newspaper. I guess you know about writing."

Cara blushed. "I'm learning."

As they sat down on the beds and cushions, Lily Vanessa eyed the dark, wooden coffee table. It did make the room friendlier, and went nicely with the beds' flowered comforters. So did the slightly worn blue floor cushions.

Jess passed the chips, bean dip, and veggies around, and Lily Vanessa noticed a giant plastic ladybug and small ladybug napkins to make the slumber party more festive. Anyone who liked ladybugs must be all right.

She relaxed a little.

Before long, Melanie and Tricia arrived, which meant all five Twelve Candles Club girls were here. She remembered their names perfectly now: Jess McColl, Cara Hernandez, Becky Hamilton, Tricia Bennett, and Melanie Lin.

Lily Vanessa felt honored to be a part of this group—

even if it was just for a while. She supposed it wasn't often that others were invited.

"Before the pizza comes," Becky said, "we need to have a short meeting." She sat down backward on the oak desk chair, and everyone else got settled.

"This special meeting of the Twelve Candles Club will now come to order," Becky began.

She turned to the green chalkboard, where names of clients and the TCCers who'd signed up to work for them were listed. "We can skip reading the minutes and the reports until Monday. Let's go over the weekend jobs. First, will Lily Vanessa need a helper to feed Miss Ida's animals tomorrow morning?"

Tricia said, "I was supposed to, but now I can't. Is there anyone else who can do it?"

Jess raised her hand. "I can. Sounds like fun!"

Lily Vanessa rolled her eyes and nodded.

Cara erased Tricia's name and chalked in "Jess."

They seemed very organized, Lily Vanessa thought.

"Anyone else?" Becky asked, looking around. No one volunteered, so she added, "Okay. Now we have several other job offers that came in since today's meeting."

While they discussed who could do other jobs, it occurred to Lily Vanessa that maybe she could start a Twelve Candles Club in L.A. She'd ask their permission.

Becky was just saying, "That concludes this special meeting of the Twelve Candles Club," when someone knocked at the door.

A boy's voice called out, "Pizza delivery! Two Morelli's deluxe pizzas!"

Jess hurried to open the door. "Perfect timing!"

Before long, giant pizzas lay on the table beside a stack of blue paper plates. Everyone sat around the table on the floor cushions, taking slices.

"Hey," Tricia said, "we need to pray."

No one offered.

Jess asked, "Lily Vanessa, would you say grace for us?"

"Me?" Lily Vanessa echoed, and Jess nodded.

She took a moment to compose herself, then prayed in firm Uncle Isaiah style.

After Lily Vanessa was finished, Tricia said, "Now that's what I call praying. Pass the pizza!"

Lily Vanessa grabbed a slice before looking up again. Maybe her prayer was different than they were used to, but that was all right, she decided.

She bit into her pizza. "Ummm . . . it's good. Let's see. Pepperoni, mushrooms, onions, sausage, green peppers, and thick-thick cheese."

"Only a good cook would examine it like that," Cara laughed. "A cook and a singer."

"That reminds me," Becky said. "The main reason for this slumber party is so we can practice our parts for Sunday morning at church."

Maybe that's why they'd invited her, Lily Vanessa thought.

Once they finished the pizza, Jess read a really good essay, "One Solitary Life," about Jesus, then the others worked on a skit about spreading God's love.

"We're dying to hear you sing," Jess said to Lily Vanessa.

"I don't have my background track with me," she said.

"I can't really do it without the track, but I promise to prac-tice tomorrow."

Tricia raised her thick, reddish gold eyebrows. "Guess we'll just have to wait to hear you on Sunday. It'll be all the better."

Lily Vanessa noticed that once the meeting, eating, and practicing ended, they started to act crazy. It was a lot like slumber parties with her friends back home. Only here they could have gone swimming in Jess's pool if the winds hadn't blown leaves, ashes, and soot across the wa-ter, leaving it filthy. They all had fun, but still they had to go to sleep by eleven, since everyone was busy the next morning.

—————

After she got home on Saturday morning, Lily Vanessa practiced with the music track while putting on her blue denim cutoffs and yellow tee. Aunt Van was already at the supermarket, and Uncle Raymond had to go to work for a while. Not that they minded her singing, but it was easier when she was alone.

At nine o'clock, Lily Vanessa biked with Jess to Miss Ida's. They left later than yesterday morning, but this way the animals wouldn't have to wait as long for Miss Ida, who was due home around noon.

Lily Vanessa glanced at Jess. "Thanks for inviting me to your slumber party. I really had a good time. And you know what I was just thinking? If it weren't for Cat, I'd never have met you guys."

"And if it weren't for Cat Woman—I mean, Miss Ida—we wouldn't have gotten to know you so well," Jess added.

It had been a terrific two weeks in Santa Rosita, Lily Vanessa thought. The only bad thing about it was the endless smell of smoke in the air from the distant fires the last few days. This morning the newscasters had said there were fires in the foothills east of L.A., too.

"The wind's getting hotter," Jess remarked as they rode onto Hill Road. "Or maybe it just feels that way up here."

"It's hotter, all right. Feels like fiery blasts from a furnace." Lily Vanessa felt her braids lift with the hot gusts. "Let's hope it won't make my voice raspy for singing tomorrow."

Two gray coyotes raced across the road.

Jess and Lily Vanessa braked fast.

"They're scared of something!" Lily Vanessa said. "Hey, look at all the quail rushing through the underbrush! And a snake! They're all scared . . . and not of us, either!"

Moments later, a siren wailed some distance behind them, and before long, they stopped their bikes by the roadside while a fire engine passed by.

"Must be a fire near here," Jess said as they rode off again.

"Let's hope it's not at Miss Ida's place!"

They pedaled harder. When they arrived, everything seemed fine, but in the distance white smoke billowed from a fire several miles away.

"That must be where the fire engine's going," Jess said.

"How do these fires get started?" Lily Vanessa asked. "It's not like we're having lightning strikes."

"Usualy it's because power lines break in the winds.

But it's arsonists sometimes," Jess answered. "You know, people who like to set fires. Mom says there's something about the Santa Ana winds that drive them crazy . . . or crazier."

"Come to think of it, that's what Uncle Raymond says, too—something about the winds loosing wildness."

A gust of hot wind pressed hard against them. This time Lily Vanessa and Jess had to strain against the wind to open the big white gate. "I wonder if Miss Ida's animals will be frightened."

"Probably," Jess answered. "Tumbles barked a lot this morning. He was very restless."

Minutes later, the cats seemed spookier than before as they crowded around their dishes. Maybe this was why she'd been sensing "excitement" lately—the "calm before the storm"!

The dogs' barking was at a higher pitch than yesterday, too.

"Thank goodness old Brutus keeps the grass and bushes trimmed," Jess remarked. "There's not many weeds or underbrush left to burn here, at least not where he's been."

Lily Vanessa wasn't so sure. "There's lots of underbrush by the driveway entrance and along the road. All around the edges of the property, too."

This morning Brutus wasn't grazing as usual. Instead he pulled hard on his chain as if to get loose.

"Maybe carrots and oats will calm him down," Lily Vanessa said. "He does like to eat. Come to think of it, I heard about a goat who ate someone's long underwear, only choking a little when he got to the elastic waistband."

Jess gave a little laugh. "Come on!"

"That's what I heard," Lily Vanessa added. "He must smell the smoke, too. Look at him pull to get loose. We'd better not move him this morning. We could give him extra oats and carrots."

"Maybe we should stay until Miss Ida gets home," Jess suggested. "If we give the animals plenty of food and water, they might be less jittery."

"I'd have to call my aunt and tell her," Lily Vanessa answered. "At least I know where the key is so we can get into the house to use Miss Ida's phone."

Quite suddenly a car went honking by on the road. "Fire!" men's voices yelled. "Fire along the road! Fire!"

For an instant, Lily Vanessa felt rooted in place, and Jess looked equally stunned. They turned and saw flames flare on the roadside grasses. Moments later, the flames grew and raced with the gusting winds. A real fire!

"Uncoil that hose up by the driveway and try to put it out," Lily Vanessa yelled. "I'll call 9–1–1!"

"Right!" Jess shouted, taking off fast toward the road.

Lily Vanessa raced to the house, grateful that Brutus had eaten away the underbrush. If only he'd eaten the tangle of it by the road!

Once inside the house, she rushed through the rooms looking for a phone. Maybe a kitchen phone! No! She glimpsed a phone in the living room, grabbed it, and dialed 9–1–1. "There's a fire by the Burston place on Hill Road in Santa Rosita."

"The street number?"

"I don't know it! High Road! High Road in Santa Rosita, south of Santa Rosita Estates!"

"We'll send someone out right away!" replied the emergency dispatcher.

She raced out toward the driveway and grabbed the nearest hose. It wouldn't reach up to the road, but if she filled this bucket with water and maybe took a shovel . . .

She ran down the driveway toward the billowing smoke. "The fire department's coming!"

Jess was backing away from the fire, the hose turned on the flames, but the small stream of water didn't do much good. Lily Vanessa threw her bucket of water onto the fire, but the flames flared up again immediately. She grabbed the shovel and began to throw dirt toward the growing line of flames. Throwing dirt helped a little, so she threw shovel after shovel of dirt at the fire.

By the road, a huge eucalyptus tree burst into flame, spreading fire around it. She and Jess backed away, still hosing and throwing dirt at the fire. Far behind them, the dogs barked hard, and Brutus bleated piteously.

At long last a siren sounded on Hill Road, and the fire engine came around the curve. "Get out of there!" a fireman yelled, waving them back toward the house. One of the men ran for the roadside fire hydrant.

Lily Vanessa and Jess retreated up the driveway.

Moments later, huge hoses of water were directed toward the flames. Another fire truck arrived, siren screaming, then a fire chief's car roared to a stop.

Lily Vanessa and Jess stood near the house watching as the firefighters battled the flames. Suddenly Miss Ida's battered tan pickup pulled up behind the fire engines, and she jumped out. She stood at the head of the driveway, clutching her heart.

"Get back! Get back!" the firemen yelled, and she backed away quickly. "Back your truck away, too!"

Miss Ida backed her pickup out of sight.

Slowly, the fire department made progress against the fire. Then finally it was out.

Lily Vanessa and Jess hurried down the driveway to reassure Miss Ida. "Your animals are fine. They're all fine."

Miss Ida still clutched her heart, but now she let out a breath of relief. Tears filled her eyes. "I don't know what I'd do without those animals. I took an early train home. Maybe God warned me something was wrong."

"These girls took care of matters just fine," a fireman told her. "If it hadn't been for them, no telling what might have happened here."

"I don't know how I can ever thank you girls," Miss Ida said. "I just don't know. . . ."

"I know how you could thank us," Lily Vanessa answered, gathering up her courage. "You could come to church tomorrow morning to hear me sing."

Miss Ida's pale blue eyes widened. "Maybe I will," she answered. "Maybe I will."

The fire captain asked, "How did the fire start?"

Jess said, "We heard a car honking up on the road, then men . . . or maybe older boys . . . yelling, 'Fire! Fire along the road!' "

The captain pushed his hat back. "Sounds like the very ones we're after. Did you see the car?"

"No. . . ."

"Did you see or hear anything else to make you suspicious?" he continued.

"Nothing," Lily Vanessa answered. "We'd just come to

feed Miss Ida's animals while she was gone."

"A good thing, too," he said again. "A very good thing."

By four o'clock that afternoon, an ocean breeze blew in across the land. The breeze blew the fires back over themselves and brought moisture in to bring the fire hazard down.

Lily Vanessa could only think, *Thank you, Lord!*

CHAPTER

10

Sunday morning, a damp breeze blew through Lily Vanessa's bedroom window. Half-awake, she heard her aunt and uncle stirring in the house, but she still felt tired from yesterday's excitement. They'd stayed with Miss Ida for a long time after the firemen left, until she'd quieted down.

Miss Ida had tried to pay them double.

"Regular pay is fine," Lily Vanessa had answered. "Fire fighting just turned out to be part of our job."

All at once Lily Vanessa sat up in bed, wide awake. This morning she was singing at Santa Rosita Community Church for Youth Sunday!

This morning!

Lord, she thought, *you helped us get through taking care of Miss Ida's animals and that fire. I know you can help me with singing this morning at church.*

Suddenly her throat felt scratchy. *Probably from inhaling*

all of that smoke the last few days. What if my voice cracks when I sing?!

She dashed from the bedroom to the kitchen. Salt. *I'll gargle with salt and hot water.*

But ten minutes later, after gargling three times, her voice was still froggy. In an hour she'd be singing at the church. . . .

She showered, inhaling steam like mad to clear her throat. It didn't help.

At breakfast Aunt Van said, "You know we'd come to pray for you if your uncle and I weren't teaching classes at our church. You said Jess McColl's father would drive you—"

"Don't worry about it," Lily Vanessa assured her. "Anyhow, you heard me sing last Sunday . . . and Ma Darice will be there." She added to her aunt, "And you did my hair wonderfully."

Her aunt smiled. "Trouble is, with your hair up like that you look too grown up to suit me, not like a twelve-year-old girl anymore."

"It makes me feel good, though," Lily Vanessa said.

"We'll be prayin' for you," Uncle Raymond promised. "Let's pray now, too."

"That my voice won't be froggy," she told him. "And that the people will be friendly to Miss Ida *if* she comes."

At eight-thirty, Mr. McColl drove his white Honda into the driveway, and Lily Vanessa hurried out. She clutched her accompaniment track for "Amazing Grace." No way could she forget that.

Jess climbed out of the front seat. "Hey, don't you look nice! I like your hair up like that."

Lily Vanessa beamed. "Thanks."

Lily Vanessa also liked her white dress with the blue swirls. If only her strappy white shoes didn't draw attention to her big feet.

"I'll ride in back with you," Jess said. "Dad can play chauffeur up front."

As Lily Vanessa climbed in, Jess introduced them, and Mr. McColl looked pleased to meet her.

"I'm eager to hear you sing," he said.

"I woke up with a frog in my throat," Lily Vanessa told him. "I hope you'll pray for me."

He backed the car from the driveway. "You've got it."

"You know what I was thinking?" Jess asked, then didn't wait for an answer. "The first time we met Miss Ida, she'd pulled the thorn from Cat's paw. She said something like, 'That cat ain't so mad now.' And she told us how bad people were to her when she went to church. Maybe she has a thorn in her heart that's turned her against people, maybe even against the Lord."

"Could be," Lily Vanessa replied. "And what about her saying how sociable goats can be if they have another goat for company . . . and how Brutus's being alone made him mean?"

Jess nodded. "Now that I think about it, that sounds like her in a way, too. Maybe not mean, but not sociable, either."

They rode along in silence for a while.

"By the way," Jess said, "the TCCers want you to be a visiting member of the club."

"Me?" Lily Vanessa asked. "A *visiting* member of the Twelve Candles Club?!"

Jess's hazel eyes shone. "You," she repeated. "With

everything that's happened . . . I mean like your knowing what to do when Jojo and Jimjim jumped on Brutus, and like your helping to fight the fire at Miss Ida's . . . we figure we've gotten to know you pretty well."

"Wow, I'm honored!"

Being "honored" sounded like something Aunt Van might say, but it was exactly what Lily Vanessa Shields meant at this moment. "I can't believe it! Thank you!"

"We hoped you might be able to stay here over Thanksgiving and Christmas vacations," Jess added.

"Maybe I can! I thought of asking if I could start a working club in L.A., but I think I'd rather come here!"

She was still astounded—and thrilled—as they drove into the church parking lot.

Then she saw the church, and her nerves took hold.

She told herself firmly that the church looked nice with its red-tiled roofs, green lawns, and red geraniums. It was just that it'd be easier if she'd visited before. Singing in strange churches was hard.

Mr. McColl dropped them off by the choir room. "I'll be praying for both of you . . . and the other kids, too. I remember Youth Sundays from when I was a boy."

Thanking him, they climbed out of the car, and Jess led the way to the rehearsal room.

At the door, a girl handed them programs.

Lily Vanessa looked inside hers.

"Amazing Grace," Lily Vanessa Shields, Solo

Seeing her name in the program made the hair on the back of her neck rise all prickly.

A short, stocky young man with broad shoulders walked over grinning and thrust a hand out to shake hers. His face glowed with the love of God. "Hi, I'm Bear, the youth minister. You must be Lily Vanessa."

She nodded and swallowed hard. "Hi."

"I enjoyed your tape so much," he added. "I'm pleased you can be in our program."

"Thanks," she replied. "I'm glad to be here." And she was glad, even though she was the only African-American in the whole room. But here came Cara, who was Hispanic, and Melanie, who was Asian—both from different ethnic groups. Ma Darice would be in the sanctuary, too.

A new thought hit. "I . . . ah . . . invited an older lady to come to the service. Miss Ida Burston. I . . . I don't know if she's a believer."

Jess stood beside her. "The Cat Woman. You know, she lives with all of those animals off Hill Road. She's lived there forever."

Bear's eyes widened. "You're kidding! Well, then, we'll ask for a miracle. I'll tell our older ladies' group to watch for her. She might enjoy them. She might even know some of them. I'll do it now. Excuse me."

Lily Vanessa nodded, then looked around the rehearsal room. Near an upright piano, Cara, Becky, Tricia, and Melanie started to practice their skit. In another corner, a guitarist and three girls rehearsed a praise song. And Jess was beginning to reread "One Solitary Life." Lots of kids rehearsing. Thirty or forty, at least.

As Bear started from the room, he turned back to Lily Vanessa. "There's the music director, Steve Monroe, with the moustache and beard. Give your accompaniment track to him. He'll make sure it's cued up right." He called out, "Hey, Steve! Here's our soloist."

It felt like everyone in the room was looking at her.

"You Lily Vanessa?" Steve Monroe asked, approaching her.

When she nodded, he said, "We've all admired your singing on the tape. Glad to have you here."

"Thanks. Here's my accompaniment track. It's an eight-bar intro."

He gave her a bright smile. "Great. I'll have it cued up the moment you stand in front of the microphone." He hesitated. "Nervous?"

"A little." Actually, her knees felt weak and quaky.

"Then you'll have to depend on Jesus, and it'll be all the better," he told her.

"That's what my Uncle Isaiah always says. He's a preacher. I sing in his church sometimes."

"Good," he said. "Glad to hear it."

Bear shouted into the room, "Time to line up to file into the sanctuary! Stay in the right order to go up easily from your pew. Lily Vanessa, you go here, after these high school kids who are giving the sermon."

Everyone arranged themselves by twos, like they'd probably learned at Wednesday night's practice. If only she'd been there, she thought, her hands clammy and her mouth dry. From being a little nervous, she zoomed to p-e-t-r-i-f-i-e-d.

"Let's go!" Bear called out.

She was paired to walk with a tense high school boy who was chewing his fingernails and looking uneasy.

Slowly, they made their way through a hallway to the back of the sanctuary. Once inside, they filed down the middle aisle between all of the people.

Hurrying along in the aisle, Lily Vanessa spotted Ma Darice sitting in the middle. Thank goodness she was wearing a dress, not one of her kente cloth African outfits.

Ma Darice gave her an ear-to-ear smile, and Lily Vanessa let a nervous smile escape in return.

Just beyond, Lily Vanessa saw Miss Ida at the side door. She wore a white blouse and blue denim skirt, and she seemed to know the two gray-haired ladies who now escorted her to a pew.

Lord, help her not to be so lonely, Lily Vanessa thought. *Lord, I pray for her salvation.*

The youth group stopped abruptly, then filed into pews in a reserved section.

Seated, Lily Vanessa eyed the pulpit and the pale green-carpeted platform. A large wooden cross hung on the white wall. She'd stand behind the microphone. She felt like harrumphing to clear her throat, but that'd make things worse. Bear walked up the steps, turned, smiled, and spoke into the microphone. "Today the youth of Santa Rosita Community Church welcome you." He spoke on, but everything seemed a haze. . . bits and pieces floating in her stage fright.

Steve Monroe stood at the keyboard, and a young woman helped the youngest kids line up on the platform. They quieted and a woman crouched down, then brought her hands up to direct them. They sang "This little light of mine, I'm gonna let it shine. . . ." The kids each waggled a pointer finger as if they were candles.

The next class sang "Jesus Loves the Little Children" . . . the next, "What A Friend We Have in Jesus." More singing . . . the TCCers' skit about loving one another . . . the guitarist and praise trio . . . Jess reading "One Solitary

Life" . . . high school kids giving the sermon.

Nice but definitely stiff, Lily Vanessa thought.

She didn't see how singing "Amazing Grace" southern gospel style could in any way fit this program. Maybe she'd pretend to be sick. No, that'd be lying. And this far up front, she couldn't escape without everyone—especially the TCCers, Ma Darice, and Miss Ida—seeing her leave.

Abruptly the high schoolers' sermons ended.

Time for her to go forward.

Move, feet, move! she told them, then hurried up the aisle. If she was jittery, it'd be picked up by the congregation and worry them. If only she could get her "self" out of the way, then God's message would come through.

Once she stood in place, her accompaniment track started its eight-bar intro. She made herself smile, mostly at the white ceiling.

Help me, Jesus! she prayed. *Please help me!*

When the music quieted, she suddenly had so much faith it was as if she were walking on water. "Aaa-aa-aaa-ma-zi-i-i-ing grace . . ."

The moment the words left her mouth, peace swept through her. No frog in her voice now.

She looked at the youth groups and TCCers. The words were connecting; they were really connecting! She filled with joyous thanksgiving, then really let her voice go. She was singing because she loved Jesus. She was singing for His glory. As a few people began to sway back and forth slightly, her spirit soared.

Through the second and third verses, her eyes touched on Ma Darice, then on Miss Ida and the older ladies around her, and suddenly she knew this was Miss Ida's day to come back to God. Everywhere people began to sway, and pure joy leapt in Lily Vanessa's soul.

She let her voice fill the sanctuary right to the end, then Steve Monroe spoke. "Let's all stand, hold hands, and sing the last verse together."

Her heart filled with wonder to see people of all descriptions singing together and holding hands across the aisles. Miss Ida held hands with the women beside her, making them look like best friends. This is how they'd all look in heaven someday, hand-in-hand and praising God together.

Jesus loves every single one of us, Lily Vanessa thought, her eyes hot with tears. *This is the wonderful excitement. Thank you, Jesus!*

How do you tell your best friends that you're moving away? Becky Hamilton is moving to another part of town, and she couldn't be more miserable. On top of that, she's still trying to get used to her new blended family—which includes Quinn, her stepbrother with an attitude.

What will the other Twelve Candles girls do without Becky close by? Will Becky still be able to be in the club? Find out in book twelve of THE TWELVE CANDLES CLUB!

Series for Middle Graders*
From Bethany House Publishers

ADVENTURES OF THE NORTHWOODS
by Lois Walfrid Johnson

Kate O'Connell and her stepbrother Anders encounter mystery and adventure in northwest Wisconsin near the turn of the century.

AN AMERICAN ADVENTURE SERIES
by Lee Roddy

Hildy Corrigan and her family must overcome danger and hardship during the Great Depression as they search for a "forever home."

JOURNEYS TO FAYRAH
by Bill Myers

Join Denise, Nathan, and Josh on amazing journeys as they discover the wonders and lessons of the mystical Kingdom of Fayrah.

MANDIE BOOKS
by Lois Gladys Leppard

With over four million sold, the turn-of-the-century adventures of Mandie and her many friends will keep readers eager for more.

THE RIVERBOAT ADVENTURES
by Lois Walfrid Johnson

Libby Norstad and her friend Caleb face the challenges and risks of working with the Underground Railroad during the mid–1800s.

TRAILBLAZER BOOKS
by Dave and Neta Jackson

Follow the exciting lives of real-life Christian heroes through the eyes of child characters as they share their faith and God's love with others around the world.

THE TWELVE CANDLES CLUB
by Elaine L. Schulte

When four twelve-year-old girls set up a business doing odd jobs and baby-sitting, they find themselves in the midst of wacky adventures and hilarious surprises.

THE YOUNG UNDERGROUND
by Robert Elmer

Peter and Elise Andersen's plots to protect their friends and themselves from Nazi soldiers in World War II Denmark guarantee fast-paced action and suspenseful reads.

* (ages 8–13)